The Famous HONEY BUNCH *Books*

By HELEN LOUISE THORNDYKE

Here is a complete list of these well-loved stories,
in order of publication.

———◆◆———

HONEY BUNCH:
HER FIRST TRIP WEST

BY

HELEN LOUISE THORNDYKE

AUTHOR OF "HONEY BUNCH: JUST A LITTLE
GIRL," "HONEY BUNCH: HER FIRST
TRIP ON THE OCEAN," ETC.

NEW YORK
GROSSET & DUNLAP
PUBLISHERS

Made in the United States of America

CONTENTS

HONEY BUNCH:
HER FIRST TRIP WEST

CHAPTER I

THE TEA PARTY

HONEY BUNCH put a lawn cover, embroidered in tiny blue and pink forget-me-nots, over Eleanor, her doll. The cover was wide enough to cover the three other dolls who were also asleep.

"There!" said Honey Bunch, with a sigh of relief. "Now we can rest a minute and then we can eat."

Honey Bunch sat down on the top step of the porch beside Ida Camp. On the next step were Kitty and Cora Williams, Anna Martin and Grace Winters. The six little girls were great friends and when a mother missed one of them, she was sure to look for her on Grove Street—Honey Bunch lived on Grove Street.

1

The dolls had been especially wakeful this afternoon, and Honey Bunch was glad to sit down and be able to talk with her visitors. She put her soft little chin on her plump little hand and remarked quietly:

"I guess I'm going West."

Ida Camp stared—she was always quiet—but Anna Martin gave a little cry.

"Good gracious me, Honey Bunch!" said Anna, who lived with her mother and her mother's old auntie and so often borrowed words from Aunt Agnes. "Goodness gracious, do you mean you're going to *die?*"

"Of course she isn't!" said Ida indignantly.

Honey Bunch looked surprised, but interested. She hadn't said a single word about dying, but Anna Martin seemed to think she had.

"Am I going to die?" Honey Bunch asked, in wonder.

"I never heard any one talk the way you do, Anna Martin!" scolded Kitty Williams. "Who said anything about dying?"

"Honey Bunch did," Anna insisted. "I

heard her—so did you! She said she is going West."

"Does every one die the minute they go West?" asked Kitty scornfully.

"I guess I know what I'm talking about!" Anna declared. "My Cousin Albert was a soldier in the war and on Memorial Day, when they have parades and things, they always talk about the soldiers who died. Only they never say they died—they say they 'went West.' And I asked Albert and he said when they died in the war, people said they went West. So if you go West you die—I guess I know!"

"Don't you die if you stay East?" asked Ida Camp.

Anna said she didn't know.

"Well, I think this is different," Honey Bunch said in her soft little voice that was always so considerate of other people's feelings. "I think this West is different, Anna. Because Daddy and Mother are going and they are going to take me with them—unless I go with my Cousin Stub."

"How far away is it?" asked Grace Winters.

"Oh, ever so far away," explained Honey Bunch. "Miles and miles. They have farms out there, but they're not like Stub's farm! I asked Daddy. These are different and they call them ranches."

"Would you rather go with your Daddy and Mother or go see Stub?" asked Cora Williams.

Honey Bunch had to think this over.

"I'd rather do both," she said frankly. "But you hardly ever can do both; so I think I'd rather go with Daddy."

Anna Martin was ready with another question.

"Where is Stub?" she demanded. "I thought she was going to be here."

"She tripped," replied Honey Bunch. "She had on a clean dress and she tripped when she carried out the cocoa pitcher after lunch; and she had to wait for a dress to be ironed because she had used hers all up. She can't wear mine—they're too small."

The front door opened with a crash and a small stocky girl tumbled headlong out on to the porch. She was dressed in a spandy clean dress, so freshly ironed that the creases still showed on the skirt and sleeves. This was Honey Bunch's Cousin Stub and you want to remember she wore a clean dress, for poor Stub led such an exciting life it seemed as though she never could keep her frocks clean very long.

"Hello!" said Stub, beaming cheerfully. "I hurried as fast as I could."

"Don't wake Eleanor," Honey Bunch cautioned, moving over so that Stub could sit beside her. "I'm telling the girls about going West."

"And Anna thought Honey Bunch meant she was going to die," giggled Cora.

"Well, soldiers always say that," Anna murmured.

Honey Bunch had been waiting for Stub to come out before she served "the party," as Norman Clark would have called the cracker sandwiches, had he been there to see them.

Norman Clark lived just back of the Mortons, and he didn't miss much that went on in Honey Bunch's yard or house, but to-day he had taken his uncle to the movies. He had told Honey Bunch that his uncle needed to be cheered up and that there was a most exciting motion picture at a theater three blocks away, which would cheer up any uncle.

"There's a fire in it and a flood and nearly everybody gets killed," Norman had announced. "My mother wouldn't take me to see it, but I think she'll let me take my uncle. He needs something like that to look at."

They had evidently gone, for Honey Bunch's party had been in progress for more than half an hour and no Norman had appeared.

"These crackers—" said Honey Bunch, spreading down a pink paper napkin on the top step and arranging seven little piles of crackers neatly on it, one pile for each corner and three down the center, "these crackers have melted marshmallows on them. You put a marshmallow on a cracker and put it in the oven and it melts like cake icing. Did you bring the chocolate drops, Stub?"

"I forgot!" said Stub. "I'll go get them now."

She jumped up and ran into the house. They heard her start up the stairs, stumble, and grunt a little as she fell down. Then the clatter of her feet sounded again and this time she must have reached the top without trouble.

"I fell upstairs," she announced cheerfully, coming back a few minutes later, crimson-faced and so breathless she could hardly talk. "I stubbed my toe. Here's the candy, Honey Bunch."

That was the reason "Stub" was called by that odd nickname. Her real name was Mary, but she was forever catching her foot in something, or stubbing her toe against something. She had numerous falls, but she never seemed to hurt herself and, as her daddy declared, she always came up smiling.

Honey Bunch took the little bag of candy

Stub had brought and arranged the flat chocolate drops in neat rows—seven rows, each
with five chocolate drops in it.

"Now we can begin," said the earnest little
hostess.

"My mother says," Ida Camp remarked, as
she took the first bite of cracker, "that something ought to be done about the traffic on
this street."

"You mean the trucks?" inquired Anna.
"You can't do anything about the trucks."

As she spoke, a huge piano van lumbered
by and the girls on the porch could feel it
shake a little.

"That's the way it is in an earthquake," said
Kitty Williams, though she had never been in
an earthquake and really didn't know how it
felt.

"All the pictures go crooked," Honey
Bunch said. "My mother has to fix them
every day."

Ida Camp, though she didn't talk a great
deal, did not give up an argument easily.
Besides, she had a brother in high school and

what he said was very important—the other
little girls admitted that, too.

"When my mother said something ought to
be done about the trucks," Ida declared, "my
brother Ned said that perhaps it could be
fixed so that Grove Street is kept for—
for—well, so that heavy trucks couldn't run
on it."

"How could they fix it?" asked Anna.

"He said there is a law for some streets,"
Ida replied. "Cars like Honey Bunch's
daddy's car could go on it, but not trucks."

"Not ice-cream trucks?" asked Honey
Bunch, in alarm.

"Well, maybe ice-cream trucks, but not
great big furniture trucks," Ida answered.

Kitty Williams said that Ebbett Avenue,
on the other side of the town, was that kind
of street.

"But I think it's because the bridge is going
to fall down," she said. "You can't have a
street fixed just because the pictures on your
walls jiggle up and down."

The crackers were all eaten now and it was

time to start on the candy. Stub ate hers, two at a time, but Honey Bunch liked to eat hers slowly and make them last. Ida tried to do everything just as Honey Bunch did, and she, too, ate her candy slowly. Anna Martin dropped one of hers down a crack between the steps and that made her a little cross, but Honey Bunch gave her one of hers right away.

"Here comes the biggest truck I ever saw!" said Grace Winters suddenly.

They had heard the noise before the car came in sight and now they looked up and saw a tremendous truck coming down the center of the street. It seemed to be almost as wide as the road and it was so high that Honey Bunch was instantly glad that she was not riding on the narrow little seat built high above the truck flooring.

"It's going pretty fast," remarked Anna.

"It's an express truck," Honey Bunch said wisely. "It goes miles and miles. Daddy told me. It goes almost as fast as a train."

The truck was so near now that the little

girls had to shout to make themselves heard. The "earthquake feeling" was rocking the porch and Honey Bunch had turned her head anxiously to see whether Eleanor was being jolted out of her comfortable place when Stub screamed.

Honey Bunch turned around just in time to see the truck stop suddenly with a great screeching of brakes. Almost at the same instant a front tire flew off and rolled directly up the lawn toward the porch. The men shouted and the girls on the lower steps jumped, Anna and Grace rolling over and over on the grass.

"Jump! Get out of the way! Run!" the men were shouting, but before Honey Bunch could tell what they were saying she knew what she was going to do.

She saw the tire—looking like a huge doughnut—rolling straight toward the steps. In another minute, it would roll right up where she and Stub were. Honey Bunch grabbed Stub by her dress and pulled as hard as she could.

"You're pulling the gathers out of my best dress!" wailed Stub.

But the tire struck the bottom step, bowled up the others as easily as though climbing porch steps was an everyday job for an automobile tire, and rolled past Honey Bunch and Stub straight for the dolls sleeping in a corner.

Crash! it struck the wall of the house and fell with a thud.

"What was that big noise?" asked Honey Bunch's mother, hurrying out, followed by Stub's mother and Mrs. Miller. They had been out in the back yard and had heard the shouting.

"What are those men running for?" asked Stub's mother. "Are any of you children hurt?"

"It's the dolls," Honey Bunch explained solemnly. "If Eleanor is killed, then she's gone West, hasn't she?"

CHAPTER II

NORMAN ASKS QUESTIONS

"EXCUSE me, Ma'am!" said a gruff voice. "Excuse me, but is anybody hurt?"

It was the driver of the truck, and his helper was close behind him, while two other men who had been on the truck were running over the lawn toward the house.

"I think no one is hurt," replied Mrs. Morton, Honey Bunch's mother. "We don't know yet what happened."

"It was a tire!" several of the little girls explained excitedly.

"Eleanor didn't go West, after all," announced Honey Bunch, coming to the railing and smiling at the truck driver, who still looked worried.

"We were having a party," said Honey Bunch to the driver, "and the tire came off your truck and rolled right up the steps and

over our table—only everything was eaten up
so that didn't matter. And I thought it rolled
over our dolls—they were asleep—but it just
missed them."

The truck driver took off his cap and
mopped his face with a red handkerchief.
The other men stood behind him and looked
at the children.

"I knew that tire was going, but I thought
it might last till the next town," said the truck
driver. "Could I get it, Ma'am?"

"Certainly," Mrs. Morton answered. "Children, step back a little, and let the man get
his tire."

"You ought to be more careful," said Mrs.
Miller severely. "I take my life in my hand
every time I cross the street, but a person has
a right to feel safe on her own front porch. If
automobiles are going to climb steps and
chase people, I think something ought to be
done about it."

Mrs. Miller washed and ironed all of
Honey Bunch's gay little frocks and she loved
Honey Bunch, too. That was what made her

so cross with the truck driver—she thought he had been careless and perhaps put her little friend in danger.

"My truck's out in the road," said the driver. "I never would let a car climb steps and chase people. I don't think it's the thing to do."

"Well, see that you don't let it act up," Mrs. Miller told him.

The driver picked up his heavy tire and saw the dolls asleep under the cover.

"Never even woke 'em up, did it?" he said. "Some children sleep through everything."

Stub nudged Honey Bunch with her elbow.

"If he's going to put on a new tire, I'd like to watch," she whispered. "Ask him if we can come look at him change the tire, Honey Bunch."

But Honey Bunch didn't have to ask, because the driver overheard Stub.

"Sure, come on," he said heartily. "There isn't much to see, but you're welcome to the best seats."

Honey Bunch knew he was joking and she smiled.

"Do you care if we go and watch him change the tire, Mother?" she asked.

"Not if you keep on the sidewalk," said her mother. "You'll have to remind Stub, Honey Bunch, for she is apt to forget when she is very much interested."

The truck had been driven to one side of the street so that it would not hold up traffic. The men went back with the rescued tire and the seven little girls hurried after them. Stub's dress was not torn at all—she said the gathers must have been sewn in it "extra hard."

"Well, anyway, I should think you'd rather have Honey Bunch pull you away from the tire, even if she did pull your gathers out, than to sit there and have an automobile tire run over you," Ida suggested.

"Oh, I would," admitted Stub. "Only I'd rather be pulled away and not have the gathers come out."

Though the men changing the tire had to

work in the sun, there was an oak tree at the
foot of the lawn, making a shady place for the
children to sit. They watched while the truck
driver and his helper got out a jack and raised
the wheel, so they could put a new tire on.

"Only it doesn't look very new," said Stub,
who always said exactly what she thought.

"It isn't," the truck driver told her. "But
it's better than the one that came off and went
to visit you."

Honey Bunch knew what Stub would say
to that, but she couldn't think of anything to
say to stop her.

"Why don't you have new tires?" asked
Stub. "My daddy does."

This didn't sound quite polite to Honey
Bunch, but she saw that the driver did not
seem to mind.

"I suppose your daddy owns his car and
buys his tires," he said. "I don't own this
truck. I drive it for the man who does own it.
And he hates to buy new tires—you know they
cost more for a big car like this than for a
pleasure car."

Stub said "Oh!" and before she had finished
thinking that over, the other tire was on and
the men were wiping their hands on a pretty
dirty cloth (Honey Bunch was glad Mrs.
Miller couldn't see that cloth—she would
want to boil it right away) and climbing up
into the high seat.

"Good-by. Glad we didn't hurt any one or
break any flower vases," said the driver, waving his hand.

"Good-by! I hope your tire will stay on,"
Honey Bunch called.

The truck started with a noise that sounded
like "a coughing thunderstorm" as Honey
Bunch described it to her daddy that evening.

Just as it lumbered past them, Norman
Clark came running down the street.

"Did the truck break down? What was
the matter with it? What were they saying
to you? Did they run over somebody?" asked
Norman breathlessly.

He always asked a dozen questions, one
right after the other. The girls were used to
it, Honey Bunch especially. Norman hated

to miss anything and not even the fact that he had cheered up his uncle that afternoon would quite make up to him for the disappointment if he should discover that something had happened in his neighborhood while he wasn't at home.

"The tire came off and it rolled up our steps and almost killed Eleanor," explained Honey Bunch. "Then the man came and got it and we came down to watch him."

"We ate everything up before it happened," Anna Martin said earnestly.

Norman looked disappointed.

"Have you seen any of the fellows?" he asked, pretending that a girls' tea party couldn't possibly interest him.

"No, we haven't," answered Honey Bunch.

"Well, what are you going to do next?" asked Norman hopefully.

"Let's talk some more about Honey Bunch's trip," Ida Camp said. "Honey Bunch is going out West, Norman—did you know that?"

"Are you? Where are you going, Honey Bunch? Are you going to-morrow? How

long are you going to stay?" sputtered Nor
man.

Honey Bunch looked a little bewildered,
as well she might.

"I don't know where we're going, but I'll
ask Mother," she said slowly. "Come on
back to the porch and I'll ask her now."

The girls and Norman followed her back
to the steps and sat down to wait while Honey
Bunch went in to find out where she might be
going.

While Honey Bunch is absent it might be
a good time to tell you a little something
about her. She was, as you know yourself, if
you have read the first book about her, a
dear little girl with blue eyes and a disposi-
tion as sunny as her hair. And her hair was
the color of real sunshine.

"Honey Bunch: Just a Little Girl," is the
title of this first book, and in that it is explained that the real name of Honey Bunch
was Gertrude Marion Morton. She lived in
the town of Barham with her daddy and her
mother and Mrs. Miller and Lady Clare.

Honey Bunch always counted them all in her
family. Though Mrs. Miller had her own
house, she was at Honey Bunch's home a
great deal, for she helped Mrs. Morton and
ironed all Honey Bunch's pretty frocks. Lady
Clare was the finest black cat you would ever
wish to see.

When Honey Bunch went visiting, as she
often did, Mrs. Miller took care of Lady
Clare. Honey Bunch went to see her Cousin
Stub, who lived on a farm, and she also visited her other cousins, the Turner twins, who
lived in New York City, and still another
cousin, Julie, who lived at the seashore. And
she had a wonderful garden and went camp-
ing with her daddy and mother and was just
about as busy a little girl as you'd find anywhere. Her daddy said so.

But it was when she went to Bermuda that
the children Honey Bunch played with in
Barham grew really excited. Honey Bunch,
you see, lived on the boat for two days and
saw a thunderstorm on the water and on the
island of Bermuda found so many wonderful

and beautiful things to see and smell and learn about that she had enough to tell the boys and girls at home—and Mrs. Miller and Lady Clare—for weeks after her return. It was in this last book, the one before this one and called "Honey Bunch: Her First Trip on the Ocean," that the story of how Lady Clare was really lost and finally found herself, is told.

Now that you're acquainted with Honey Bunch Morton, we'll go back to the children waiting on the porch for her.

"I want Honey Bunch to come and see me," said Stub. "She could come and see me while her daddy and mother are out West."

"I think it would be more exciting to go out West," Norman replied frankly. "She's been to see you."

Stub wasn't in the least offended.

"Well, I would rather go West, too, I think," she admitted. "But if I wasn't going West, I would rather visit one of my cousins."

Honey Bunch came running back just then, but before she could tell them what she had asked her mother three boys shouted from the sidewalk.

"Hello!" they called. "Is Norman here?"

Norman could be seen very plainly—he was sitting on the railing—so this question was really intended as a greeting.

"Come on up," called the hospitable Honey Bunch. "Mother says we are going to Three Rock Ranch."

Teddy and Elmer Gray and Albert Barnes galloped up the walk and looked, so Kitty Williams said, as though they were going to the movies.

"Where's the ranch?" they asked eagerly.

"A ranch is a farm," said Stub scornfully. "We live on a farm. I don't see why any one calls a farm a ranch."

The boys didn't care whether it was a farm or a ranch, but they were very anxious to know where Three Rock Ranch was.

"I'll find it on the map for you, if you have a map," Teddy Gray offered.

"Oh, I have a map," said Honey Bunch proudly. "I have a book almost like Ida's

brother's geography book. Daddy bought it
for me when we came home from Bermuda."

"Come on in and let's find the place," Stub
urged. "I'll roll up the curtains."

Stub delighted to let the shades in the living room go up with a snap. She did it,
whether any more light was needed or not.
Now she pranced ahead of Honey Bunch and
the others and had the shades at the three windows rolled up to the top before they reached
the living room.

Honey Bunch had her own books on her
own shelf. The lowest shelf of the book case
was hers. She knew the geography book, too
—it had a red cover.

"Be sure you get a map that is out West,"
said Norman Clark. "A map that isn't out
West won't be a bit of good."

CHAPTER III

MAP TRAVELS

"How can I find Three Rock Ranch if I can't even see the map?" demanded Teddy Gray.

Seven girls, even little ones, and four boys, even thin little boys, take up a good deal of room, you know. And if eleven children all try to see a page of one book at the same time, you know without being told that the book is likely to be torn in two, or else some of the children will be so crowded that they cannot see the page.

"Put it flat on the floor, Honey Bunch," said Anna Martin. "We can see it, if it's on the floor. Like this—" and she opened the book and put it on the rug.

"I think," Kitty Williams said seriously, "this is a map of the East."

Honey Bunch looked worried.

"There are some more," she answered. "All through the book. There must be a map of the West somewhere, Kitty."

"Here it tells about growing rice in China," said Norman. "I'll read you about it."

"We aren't talking about China," Cora Williams replied. "We're talking about where Honey Bunch is going."

"If she doesn't come to visit me," said Stub.

"I can find Three Rock Ranch, but I have to have the right kind of a map," Teddy Gray declared.

Cora Williams turned over the page where Norman was placidly reading about how rice is grown in China.

"There's a map!" she said. "That's a good map, isn't it, Honey Bunch? I guess you can find the West on this map if you look, Teddy."

"It has the Atlantic Ocean," objected Teddy.

"And New York and Maine—this must be an East map," Albert Barnes said, looking over Cora's shoulder.

"You have to go West on the map, too," explained Elmer Gray, who was almost as quiet as Ida Camp. "How far West are you going, Honey Bunch?"

"I—I—I'm not sure," Honey Bunch murmured.

"Well, you'll go as far as this red line, I guess," said Elmer. "Here's Forked Ranch —this must be near where you're going, Honey Bunch."

The boys lay flat on the floor and pored over the map, while the girls had to be content with the printing and the figures on the page margins.

"Do you see Three Rock Ranch?" asked Honey Bunch, when she had waited several minutes.

"No-o. But here is Tombstone," Elmer announced cheerfully. "I wouldn't mind going to a place called Tombstone."

"I'd rather go to Medicine Hat," said Norman Clark. "Maybe they make gallons and gallons of medicine there and I could stir it with a wooden spoon."

"It wouldn't be so funny if they made you take it," Anna Martin suggested. "You make an awful fuss when you take cod-liver oil, Norman."

"I'm going to Deadwood," declared Stub, who didn't believe that girls should be entirely shouldered out of the way by boys and who had managed to get hold of a corner of the map page with a plump thumb and forefinger.

Grace Winters giggled.

"Going West sounds kind of solemn, doesn't it?" she suggested. "I should think you'd pick out a nice, cheerful name. I wouldn't go to places that sound so—so kind of unhappy."

Honey Bunch couldn't read the little fine names printed on the map—she couldn't read, anyway, unless someone helped her—but she pointed her finger to a black speck.

"Maybe that's Three Rock Ranch," she suggested.

"No, it isn't," said Teddy. "That's Broken Foot."

"Who names the towns?" Stub demanded.
"I wouldn't name towns such funny names.
But then, I guess people who call farms
ranches are queer, anyway."

"My father says lots of things sound queer
when you're not used to them," Teddy Gray
declared. "I don't believe the folks who live
in Broken Foot or Tombstone think those
names are funny. Maybe Barham sounds
funny to them."

Honey Bunch still hoped to find Three
Rock Ranch. She put her small nose almost
on the map and was tracing the pink and yellow and green outlines with a pointed little
finger, when something large and soft and
black dropped down in front of her, just miss-
ing her yellow head.

"Why, Lady Clare!" said Honey Bunch, in
surprise.

"Where did she come from?" Kitty Williams asked, looking up at the ceiling as
though she rather expected to see a hole there.
"I didn't see her before, did you?"

Honey Bunch had lifted the big cat

into her lap and was stroking her softly.

"She must have been on top of the book-case," she explained. "She climbs up there to go to sleep, sometimes. She must have heard us talking—and maybe she wants to go West, too. Do you, Lady Clare?" added Lady Clare's little mistress.

The cat only purred and Anna Martin said that cats didn't like to travel.

"She likes to stay with Mrs. Miller," said Honey Bunch comfortably. "Maybe she wouldn't like it on a ranch at all."

"No, I don't believe she would," Stub declared. "On a farm the cats can play in the barn, but goodness only knows whether there are any barns on a ranch."

Stub, you see, was anxious for Honey Bunch to go back to Broad Acres with her. Broad Acres was the name of the farm that Stub's daddy owned and where she lived.

Even after the other children had gone home that afternoon, Stub kept trying to persuade Honey Bunch that she would have

much more fun on the farm than at Three
Rock Ranch.

"Your daddy and mother can go, but you
come to see me," urged Stub.

"I would like to come and see you and
Aunt Carol," Honey Bunch said seriously,
"if Mother and Daddy would come, too. But
if they are going West, I would rather go
West, too."

And that was the way it was finally settled.

"I can't put this trip off any longer," said
Mr. Morton to Stub's mother, who had told
him how delighted she would be to take
Honey Bunch home with her. "It's a business trip that must be attended to. Edith likes
the idea of visiting the ranch and neither one
of us is willing to leave Honey Bunch behind. If we had six little girls we might leave
one or two, but when you have only one,
Carol, you can't help worrying unless she is
where you can see her every minute."

Stub's pretty mother laughed and said she
felt that way about Stub, too.

The next day she and Stub went back to

the farm and the Morton family began to get
ready for their trip in "dead earnest," as Mrs.
Miller observed.

"What is dead earnest?" asked Honey
Bunch. "If going West is dying dead, and
Deadwood is the name of a town and Tomb-
stone is——"

"Merciful goodness me, Honey Bunch!"
said Mrs. Miller. "You give me the creeps!"

That showed how upset she was. Sometimes she said "Goodness" and now and then
she said "Merciful goodness," but when Mrs.
Miller said "Merciful goodness me!" you
could tell she was very much upset.

"Stop talking about such things as tomb-
stones," she told Honey Bunch. "When I say
we're getting ready in dead earnest, all I
mean is—all I mean is—well, all I mean is
we're getting ready."

"Yes, I see," said Honey Bunch gravely.
"And I'd better be getting Eleanor's clothes
ready in dead earnest."

She was so interested in trying to decide
whether Eleanor—her largest and best loved

doll—should wear a pink or blue dress on the train that she didn't hear her daddy call her a few minutes later.

"Honey Bunch!" Daddy Morton called again. "Oh, can any one tell me what has become of a little girl named Honey Bunch?"

"Here she is!" cried Honey Bunch, running out into the hall.

"What were you doing that you didn't hear me the first time?" Daddy Morton asked. "I can't find Mother and I thought you would know where she is."

"I'm getting Eleanor's clothes ready in dead earnest," said Honey Bunch, "and Mother has gone over to say good-by to Mrs. Farriday."

"How about saying good-by to Norman Clark in dead earnest?" Daddy Morton suggested, his eyes twinkling. "I hope you won't forget that, Honey Bunch."

"I won't," promised Honey Bunch. "I meant to do it, anyway."

The Farridays lived on one side of the Mortons and the Perkins family lived on the other side. Norman Clark's back yard touched the Morton back yard so Honey Bunch always counted him as a next-door neighbor. There were no little boys or girls in the Farriday or Perkins houses, so Honey Bunch did not have to say good-by to the neighbors next door; her mother did it for her.

Mrs. Miller had been down in the laundry when Mr. Morton came home and called to Honey Bunch. She could not hear anything that went on upstairs when she was down there, and she was much surprised when she came up with a basket of clean clothes an hour later and Honey Bunch told her that Daddy had come in and gone again.

"Well, there's his handkerchiefs, ironed ex-actly as he likes to have 'em," said Mrs. Miller proudly. "And if I do say it as shouldn't, your dresses never looked better, Honey Bunch. Your mother says you've got a new dark blue silk dress to wear on the train."

"With bloomers," Honey Bunch added, also proudly. "If I do say it as shouldn't, I think new dresses are lovely, Mrs. Miller."

"I declare, Honey Bunch," said Mrs. Miller, laughing, "I'll miss hearing you talk more than anything else. I wish you'd come and stay with me while your mother and daddy go traveling off to this queer place."

"Oh, I couldn't!" Honey Bunch answered in great alarm. "My mother needs me, Mrs. Miller. But I will send you a post-card."

Mrs. Miller said that would help and then she went back to the laundry to iron more dresses and to tell Lady Clare that she meant to take her home with her that night. Lady Clare loved to stay with Mrs. Miller. And no wonder, because she had liver and cream to eat and a red cushion with yellow flowers on it to sleep on; but the big black cat certainly did hate to be carried in a basket to the washerwoman's house. Still, Lady Clare behaved very nicely about it and did not make any more fuss than she could help.

Honey Bunch decided that Eleanor should wear the pink dress and she put it on her, and also the white cape with pink flowers on it which Stub's mother had made for the doll to travel in, and then, looking out of the window, she saw Norman Clark on the fence and she went down into the yard to say good-by to him.

"Are you going?" said Norman, as soon as he saw Honey Bunch. "What train are you going on? Has your mother packed the trunk yet?"

"I should think you'd wear that fence out, Norman Clark," Mrs. Miller called disapprovingly, from the doorway of the laundry.

CHAPTER IV

WHAT THE BOYS WANTED

NORMAN CLARK always sat upon the fence, and really Mrs. Miller should have been used to it by this time. But she didn't like to see him "jiggle" the boards, and as Norman simply couldn't sit on top of the fence and not jiggle, he and Mrs. Miller had rather frequent arguments.

"The fence is all right," said Norman now to Mrs. Miller. "Say, Honey Bunch, I don't suppose you could bring me a pistol when you come back?"

"A pistol?" repeated Honey Bunch doubtfully.

"Yes, they always have pistols out West," Norman assured her. "I thought it would be nice if you brought me one."

Mrs. Miller was taking a dry tablecloth off the line and she sniffed.

"Your mother would think a pistol was nice!" said Mrs. Miller, and the way she said it you knew right away that she meant Mrs. Clark would think a pistol was not nice at all.

"I will look around in dead earnest," Honey Bunch promised. "But if I can't find a pistol, will something else do, Norman?"

"Well, a pony would be all right," admitted Norman. "But I was trying to think of you, Honey Bunch. A pony would be hard to carry."

Honey Bunch was sure she couldn't carry a pony, but she promised to bring Norman something, and that pleased him. When he heard she was going the very next day, he said he'd go around with her and help her say good-by to the other boys and girls.

"I should think you'd have a bon voyage party," said Norman, as he and Honey Bunch started off.

"Ida told me about that," Honey Bunch explained. "You have to go on a ship to have a bon voyage party. When you go on a train it isn't a voyage."

"What is it?" asked Norman promptly.

"It's a trip," Honey Bunch said.

"Can't you have a trip party?" suggested Norman.

"My, no!" Honey Bunch answered. "I never heard of a trip party!"

They found Ida Camp on her porch and she said she would come along and help Honey Bunch say good-by, too.

It was odd, but every one of the boys wanted a pistol. They seemed to think that Honey Bunch might find the pistols growing on the bushes out West and that it would be no trouble at all for her to stop and pick a few, to bring home to her friends in the East.

Elmer Gray wanted a pistol and so did his brother, Teddy, and Albert Barnes and even a friend of Albert's, whom Honey Bunch had never seen before. His name was Fred Gates and he said he would rather have a pistol than anything else in the world.

"Just to play with," he added, as though he thought Honey Bunch might suspect him of wishing to frighten people with his pistol.

Of course Cora and Kitty Williams and Anna Martin didn't want any pistols. They were too polite to ask Honey Bunch to bring them anything, but when she said she would try to find something they would like, they couldn't help looking pleased.

"It isn't polite to ask for presents," declared Kitty; "but it is nice to get presents."

Honey Bunch thought so, too, and that night at dinner she told her daddy she thought they ought to take an empty basket with them.

"I have to get five pistols," Honey Bunch explained, "and something nice for Kitty and Cora and Ida and Anna, and Mary and Fannie Graham, too. So I will need something to carry the presents in, Daddy."

Mrs. Morton looked startled and she said, "Five pistols!" before Mr. Morton could speak.

"What do you want with five pistols?" asked Mr. Morton the next moment.

"I don't want them," Honey Bunch answered quickly. "The boys want them. I

think they want them in dead earnest,
Daddy."

Honey Bunch was used to seeing her daddy
laugh. He laughed a great deal but even
when he laughed about things she said, she
did not mind. Now he looked at Mother and
laughed as though he never would stop.

"We won't take a basket, Honey Bunch, for
two reasons," he said at last. "One is that we
can't be bothered with extra baggage, and the
other is that I don't believe they'll let us bring
back pistols. I think they need pistols out
West more than they do in Barham. We'll
look around for something else."

Honey Bunch was secretly relieved. She
knew about Fourth-of-July pistols and she
didn't like them herself and she knew that if
Norman had one he would probably frighten
Lady Clare into fits. Not that he would
mean to, but Norman just couldn't help play-
ing cowboy and chasing things, if he had a
pistol to play with.

Mrs. Miller took Lady Clare home with
her that night. She told her the cushion was

waiting for her and that she should have
cream for breakfast and boiled liver for
lunch.

"You'll live like a queen," Mrs. Miller
told Lady Clare, who blinked her beautiful
green eyes and acted as though she was perfectly willing to live like a queen.

Honey Bunch was used to traveling by this
time—for a small girl she had made a good
many journeys. She knew how trunks were
packed and how the express man would bump
them down the steps, no matter how much
your mother asked him to be careful.

She knew how the house looked with all
the windows closed and the shades drawn
down and no Lady Clare purring lazily in one
of the comfortable chairs. As soon as the
house was in order to leave, Honey Bunch
liked to go. She could not have explained it
very well, but it didn't seem like her house
when it was so still that you could hear the
clocks ticking distinctly in every room.

Norman Clark was waiting on the curb the
next morning when the taxi came for Honey

Bunch and her mother and daddy. Mrs. Miller said Norman never missed anything; and there wasn't much he didn't see, for a fact. He was a wide-awake boy and he couldn't help being tremendously interested in everything his neighbors did. He was very good-natured, too, in spite of his curiosity, and though he seldom went traveling himself, it never entered his head to be jealous of his friends who had pleasant and exciting adventures.

"Don't forget the pistol," he said to Honey Bunch, who came out first, with Eleanor in her arms.

"A pistol or something else," Honey Bunch reminded him firmly. "I don't think I can get a pistol, Norman; you mustn't set your heart on it."

That was what Mrs. Miller said when Honey Bunch hoped it wouldn't rain on a certain day. If you set your heart on a certain kind of weather, Mrs. Miller said, it would almost always be another kind.

The taxi man smiled at Honey Bunch and

opened the door of his cab, so she thought he expected her to get in and wait for Daddy and Mother. He helped her up the step and Norman sat down on the running board.

"Have you a pistol?" he asked the taxi man.

"Good grief, that I have not!" answered the taxi man. "I hope you don't want me to lend you my pistol that I haven't got?"

"Well, no," Norman admitted. "I was only asking. Honey Bunch is going out West and maybe she will bring me a pistol when she comes back."

"Then I'll stay off this street for the rest of my days," said the taxi man. "I'm old and wise and I never go within seven blocks of a house when I know a boy has a pistol."

"But Norman's mother might want to go to the seashore," Honey Bunch said. "She always takes a taxi to the station, when she is going to the seashore. Wouldn't you even come and get her?"

"Not if I knew this lad had a pistol," said the taxi man firmly. "Any one who wants me to drive 'em, can't be flourishing a pistol

around. So you take my advice and forget to
bring a pistol back with you."

"Well, I don't believe Daddy will let me,
anyway," Honey Bunch explained, "because
all the boys want one and five pistols are too
many and they'd make an awful noise. And
we are not taking a basket to bring them home
in, either, because Daddy says that extra baggage is too heavy."

"Here they come now!" said Norman, getting up from the running board.

Mr. and Mrs. Morton came down the steps,
Mr. Morton carrying the two bags, and the
taxi man helped Honey Bunch's mother up
the step and then Daddy Morton told him to
take them to the station and he got in and
the door closed with a bang.

"Good-by, Norman!" called Honey Bunch,
waving her hand.

"Good-by, Honey Bunch!" Ida Camp
called from her porch. She lived across the
street.

"Don't forget the pistol—maybe!" shouted
Norman.

The taxi man honked his horn and drove away as fast as he could go. Perhaps he was afraid that Norman might run all the way to the station after them, reminding Honey Bunch about the pistol.

"Now we're going to Three Rock Ranch!" announced Honey Bunch, settling herself contentedly on one of the little front seats, with Eleanor on her lap.

"Not straight there," Daddy Morton said quickly. "We have to go to Chicago first."

"Have I ever been to Chicago?" asked Honey Bunch, with interest.

"You've passed through the city, haven't you?" her daddy answered. "No, I don't believe you have. Where *have* you been, Honey Bunch?"

Honey Bunch counted on her fingers.

"To New York," she began. "That was fun. And to Stub's and the seashore and to camp and on an automobile trip, and to Bermuda. But I don't think I've been to Chicago."

"You haven't, dearest," said Mrs. Morton.

"Daddy is teasing—and here is the station
and we'd better be thinking about getting a
train instead of teasing each other."

The taxi man said he hoped Honey Bunch
would have a good time and Honey Bunch
told him truthfully that she always had a
good time. She turned around at the station
door and he was waiting to wave to her.
Honey Bunch did hope that he would come
and take Norman Clark's mother to the seashore when she was ready to go.

The big platform was crowded with people
waiting for the train. One end was piled high
with trunks and bags and suitcases and there
was a little dog tied by a rope to one of the
platform seats.

"Do you suppose he is going to Chicago?"
said Honey Bunch, staring at the little dog
who blinked at her.

"No, he's going to Mount Berry," a boy
standing near by answered.

The boy was quite grown up—he looked as
old as Ned, Ida Camp's brother who went to
high school.

"Will he like it there?" asked Honey Bunch.

"Sure he will!" the grown-up boy replied. "He'll find plenty of cats to chase."

"Oh, dear!" sighed Honey Bunch. "Don't let him chase cats. They don't like to be chased. Lady Clare gets all ruffled up if a dog chases her. But sometimes she scratches them on the nose."

"Is Lady Clare your cat?" the boy asked.

Honey Bunch nodded and she had just begun to tell him how Lady Clare looked when a man in a blue uniform began to shout.

"Chicago Limited!" he shouted through a horn. "Chicago Limited! First stop Fancher! First stop Fancher!"

He said a great deal more, and everything he said twice, though Honey Bunch couldn't understand it all, he spoke so fast. Still, she thought it was very good of him to say things twice, because if you didn't hear it the first time, you might the second time.

"Three cars ahead," said the conductor, who looked at the tickets Mr. Morton held out to him.

The train was slowing down, but it had not stopped yet. Honey Bunch looked at the conductor reproachfully.

"It's six cars long now," she murmured, "and there's one more—that makes seven."

"Hey?" shouted the conductor loudly. "Hey? I didn't hear you."

The long train had stopped by now and Honey Bunch could feel the heat from the wheels. Her daddy had hold of her hand and he had not heard what she said to the conductor. He hurried her along and Honey Bunch found herself stepping on a little stool the porter put down for her before she could make any one understand that she had not finished her conversation.

"I have to go back and tell the conductor what I said," she insisted. "He didn't hear me."

"That wasn't a conductor, dear," said her mother. "That man in uniform was one of

the station men, but he isn't a conductor.
What were you saying to him?"

"About the three cars ahead," Honey
Bunch explained, hopping up the train
steps, because the porter so evidently expected her to go right on. "He said three
cars ahead, Mother and I counted seven.
And now he'll be wondering what I said to
him, won't he?"

"He's busy," said Mrs. Morton comfortably. "He'll forget about it in a minute.
And I think he knew just about what section
of the train would stop here where we were
standing and what car would be three cars
ahead of us. Train men know their trains
so well that they can tell almost exactly where
they will stop every day."

CHAPTER V

TRAIN FRIENDS

HONEY BUNCH thought about this while the porter was finding their seats for them and getting them nicely settled. The Mortons would not sleep on this Chicago train. Though Honey Bunch had been disappointed at first when she heard that, her mother told her that another train they would take—from Chicago to Three Rock Ranch—would have sleeping cars attached and that they would spend three nights on that train.

"You'll have plenty of traveling before we see the ranch, Honey Bunch," her daddy promised the little girl. "It isn't the easiest place in the world to reach, but we globe-trotters like to cover a good deal of ground, don't we, Bunch of Sweetness?"

"Oh, yes," said Honey Bunch, smiling.

Then Honey Bunch found that the reason

she and Mother and Daddy had not taken a sleeping-car on the Chicago train was because Daddy wished to get off before they reached that big city and stay over night at another place where he could see an old friend for a few hours.

Honey Bunch was sound asleep when they reached this place, and she knew nothing about it until the next morning. But bright and early they again got a train for Chicago, and this time Honey Bunch knew exactly what was going on and was greatly interested.

The very first thing the experienced Honey Bunch always did when she found herself on a train, was to look about her and see if there were any other children in the car. She liked little girls her own age best, but boys, unless they were the teasing kind, were nice, too, and older children could be the nicest kind of friends, Honey Bunch had learned.

But in this car there wasn't a single boy or girl, little or big. Sitting directly across from her chair was an old lady who looked as though she might be a grandma. In the chair next to her was an old gentleman who looked as though he must be somebody's grandpa. The rest of the people were "just people," as Honey Bunch would have told you. Most of them were reading newspapers, though one lady was knitting and one man had gone to sleep with his hands folded neatly across his vest.

"He must have been saying his prayers," Honey Bunch whispered to Mother.

The old lady across the aisle heard her and looked over and smiled.

"I wish you'd introduce me to your doll," she said to Honey Bunch. "If you will, I'll introduce you to mine."

Honey Bunch's blue eyes opened wide. She had never heard of an old lady with a doll. Besides, she couldn't see a doll anywhere. If it was in a trunk in the baggage car, it might be a large doll, but surely an ordinary-sized doll would be out in plain sight where every one could see it!

"Go over and tell her about Eleanor, dear," said Mrs. Morton.

Honey Bunch straightened Eleanor's hat and crossed the aisle.

"My doll's name is Eleanor," said Honey Bunch clearly. "She is my favorite doll. This is her best dress and my Aunt Carol made the cape for her."

"How do you do, Eleanor?" said the old lady politely. "I'm delighted to know you. I am Grandma Elder and that is Grandpa Elder, smiling at you in the next chair."

Honey Bunch turned and saw the old gentleman who looked like a grandpa smiling at her and Eleanor.

"I'm Honey Bunch," said the little girl politely. "My real name is Gertrude Marion Morton, but every one calls me Honey Bunch."

"I don't wonder," said Grandma Elder. "I have four little granddaughters and they have blue eyes just like yours."

"What are their names?" asked Honey

Bunch, who loved to hear about other little girls.

"The oldest one is named Anna, and the next is Kitty and the two youngest are Frances and Jane," said Grandma Elder. "Would you like to see the presents I am taking home to them?"

Well, of course Honey Bunch would—she dearly liked to see presents and especially those for little girls like herself. Her eyes danced as the old gentleman took down a bag from the rack over her head and opened it.

"You'll have to tie them all up again," said Honey Bunch thoughtfully.

"Bless you, I don't mind that," said Grandpa Elder. "I like to unwrap presents and I like to tie them up again. There's the doll, Mother."

Grandma Elder took the package he handed her and untied the pink string.

"This is the doll I call mine," she explained. "I thought I could call it mine until I give it to Jane. There!"

She opened a box and held it out to Honey Bunch.

"I'll hold Eleanor for you while you look at it," the old lady said.

The box held a little doll—not more than three inches high. And there was everything a doll could possibly want or use in the box with her. Honey Bunch counted four dresses, four hats, one coat and a cape. There were shoes and stockings, a kimono, hair brushes, combs, a little leather purse to take shopping, and a little book just the right size for a doll to read.

"Isn't it lovely!" cried Honey Bunch, in delight.

"I thought Jane would like it," Jane's grandma answered. "She likes little things. All her toys are small. Frances is different; she likes to play with the kind of toys boys like."

Honey Bunch nodded.

"Grace Winters does, too," she said, "and so does my Cousin Stub. My Cousin Stub says that boys' toys don't break so easily."

Grandpa Elder laughed as he began to tie
up the doll box.

"That may be the reason Frances likes such
things," he said. "She does break a good
many things."

Honey Bunch took the box Grandma Elder
handed her and opened it carefully. In it
she found what she thought was a set of
blocks, but Grandma Elder explained that
they were not blocks.

"It's a construction set," she said. "The
girl at the toy counter told me you can make
a train or an automobile or a milk wagon,
out of these pieces of wood."

"I would rather make a milk wagon," said
Honey Bunch decidedly.

"Well, I don't think I could make an automobile, but Frances likes mechanics and she
may be able to do it," Grandma Elder declared. "Now, Father, where is the present
we bought for Kitty?"

The old gentleman untied a third package
and handed it to Honey Bunch with a little
smile.

"Oh-h, how perfectly lovely!" she cried, as soon as she saw what it was.

For Kitty's present was—what do you think? A kitty! Yes'm, a little toy cat with long silky white hair and yellow glass eyes. She wore a blue ribbon and on the ribbon was a little silver bell. She looked exactly like a live cat, and Honey Bunch kissed her pink nose because she couldn't help it.

"Is it because her name is Kitty?" she asked eagerly.

"You mean, is that the reason we bought the cat?" asked Grandma Elder.

"Well, partly," she continued. "The real reason is, that Kitty is so devoted to cats. She is always bringing home sick cats and lame cats and the great grief of her life is that her mother will not let her take a cat to bed with her. I thought if we brought her a nice, clean toy cat, she could have it in bed with her at night and perhaps she won't tease to be allowed to have a live cat in her room."

Honey Bunch liked Kitty's present better than any of the others. Not even the little silver purse that was to go to Anna pleased her half as much as that white toy cat.

Grandma Elder, who knew a great deal about little girls as all grandmas do, saw how much she liked the cat and she said that Honey Bunch should have it to play with until they reached Chicago.

"No, she won't get it dirty," she said, when Mrs. Morton pointed out that a white cat might get soiled from the coal smoke and cinders that will sift into the train, no matter how careful the train folk are to keep everything screened. "The cat won't get dirty, because we haven't such a long ride now. And, anyway, if it should get dirty I can easily have it cleaned."

So Honey Bunch had the cat to play with and she had the nicest time with it. She could hold it on her lap or put it on the window sill and the conductor pretended to be much shocked when he saw it and declared that all animals must ride in the baggage car.

"But this is a toy cat," explained Honey Bunch. "Feel it."

The conductor took the pretty toy cat and shook it gently.

"That's the way I always tell," said he. "If you shake a live cat, she scratches you, but a toy cat doesn't scratch. So this must be a toy cat and you may keep her in this car."

Honey Bunch smiled her thanks and she and the cat kept each other company until the train pulled into the big Chicago station. Then Grandpa and Grandma Elder said good-by, for they lived in Chicago and were going straight home to the four little grand-daughters. But of course the Mortons had not much more than started on their long journey.

"I certainly would hate to have to mop this floor," said Honey Bunch, feeling like a very small girl indeed as she held fast to Mother's hand and saw crowds of people hurrying past her in the huge waiting room of the enormous station.

Mrs. Miller always looked at the floors wherever she went and she always thought about her mop and bucket. There was a colored man mopping in one corner of the room now, and of course as soon as Honey Bunch saw him she thought of Mrs. Miller.

"We have several hours to wait," announced Mr. Morton, "and I think we'd better have lunch—I've heard that the charlotte russe is very good here."

Honey Bunch and her daddy doted on charlotte russe and when they were seated at a little round table just right for three, Mr. Morton asked the waiter about the charlotte russe before he even mentioned soup or any of the things that are good for you and make you grow.

"The charlotte russe is very fine to-day, sir," declared the waiter. "I don't know when we've had it any better. Stands up fine and white, sir, and there's a red cherry on the top of every one."

Goodness, perhaps that didn't make Honey Bunch hungry! Mrs. Morton laughed but she said she'd have the same dessert, too. Other things were ordered, and after that

very good lunch had been eaten and it was
time for the charlotte russe, the waiter
brought a charlotte russe for Honey Bunch
that had two big fat cherries on it, instead of
one.

"I'd like to see about getting a letter off to
New York," said Mr. Morton when they had
left the dining room and the waiter had said
he hoped to have the pleasure of serving
Honey Bunch another charlotte russe when
she came home from the West. "If I can
find a public stenographer, can you and
Honey Bunch amuse yourselves for half an
hour, Edith?"

"Of course. We'll walk around and look
at everything there is to be seen," said Mrs.
Morton. "Perhaps we'll buy something to
play with on the train."

CHAPTER VI

THE BIG STATION

"Where'll we find Daddy?" asked Honey Bunch anxiously.

"Right by this door," her daddy answered promptly. "I'll come back here and wait for you. We'll check the bags, so they won't be on our minds, and we have so much time before the train goes that no one need worry. And, oh, Honey Bunch, I saved something for you."

Honey Bunch "saved" things for her daddy and he saved things for her. Sometimes when he came home at night, he would find a pretty maple leaf at his plate or acorns (he could make the dearest little tea sets from acorns) or perhaps a crayon drawing Honey Bunch had made.

Then for Honey Bunch he saved all the fascinating things that seem to grow in offices

down town. Colored papers and pencils,
rubber bands, pretty blotters and calendars—
there were dozens of little presents like these
that he brought home to Honey Bunch. He
also saved for her every new penny he found
in his change. The old, dull or dirty looking pennies did not count, but brand-new,
shining pennies that looked as though they
were made of solid gold he brought home to
his little daughter.

"When I bought our tickets the agent gave
me ten new pennies," said Mr. Morton. "I
have been keeping them for you—here you
are," and he put ten shining copper cents into
Honey Bunch's hand.

She had a new blue purse on a chain and
there was a new ten-cent piece already in it.
Honey Bunch felt most important and almost
grown up with so much money making a
pleasant tinkle in her purse. She also had a
blue and white handkerchief and a little
round cake of chocolate wrapped in tinfoil.
Grandpa Elder had given her that on the
train.

"If you come back before I do, wait for me right by this door," said Mr. Morton, hurrying off and getting so mixed up with the other hurrying folk that Honey Bunch couldn't tell in which direction he really did go.

"What is a public—a public—you know, Mother?" asked Honey Bunch earnestly.

"Well, you know Miss Mead in Daddy's office?" Mrs. Morton asked. "She is Daddy's stenographer and writes his letters; but she doesn't write letters for any one else. A public stenographer doesn't work in any one office—she has an office or a desk of her own, and she writes letters for every one who asks her."

"In the station?" asked Honey Bunch. "Where 'bouts, Mother?"

"I don't see her doing it," Mrs. Morton admitted. "But somewhere, in a quiet place, there must be an office with a public stenographer in it. You see hundreds of busy men—like Daddy—have to wait in this station between trains, and they can get their

letters written and mailed if there is a stenographer to write for them. If Daddy
waited till we reached the ranch, his letter
might be so late that it wouldn't do any
good."

Honey Bunch thought she understood, but
she decided to look carefully and see if she
couldn't see a public stenographer writing
letters.

There certainly was a great deal to see in
that huge station. Honey Bunch and her
mother couldn't seem to get past the flower
stand, which was nearest the door where Mr.
Morton had left them. Honey Bunch knew
about flowers—hadn't the snapdragons from
her own little garden won the first prize at
the Barham flower show?—and she could
name almost all the flowers the pretty girl
at this stand had for sale.

"Ida would love that little pink vase," said
Honey Bunch, looking wistfully at a rose-
colored glass vase with a handle of gold and
cream. "Could we buy it, Mother?"

"It's beautiful, dear," Mrs. Morton an-

swered. "But you know how easily glass
breaks. We would have to take great care
of the vase and perhaps carry it all the way
to the ranch and back again, to make sure it
was safe. I'm sure we can find something
Ida will like just as well and which will not
be so much trouble on our journey."

"Yes, it might get cracked," agreed Honey
Bunch. "Do you suppose they have any pistols in this station, Mother?"

"I don't believe they do," Mrs. Morton
said, smiling. "In fact, I'm afraid Norman
will have to make up his mind to accept some
other gift. What ever made him say he
wanted a pistol, Honey Bunch?"

"He says he has always wanted one," declared Honey Bunch. "He wants a pony, too.
But I can't put a pony in the trunk."

"Norman will have to take a trip West
himself some day," Mrs. Morton said. "See
the funny little baby, Honey Bunch."

A few feet from Honey Bunch, a tired
family stopped for a moment's rest. The
women wore bright colored shawls over their

heads and one carried a tiny baby, also wrapped in a shawl. The men wore odd looking hats and their coats did not seem to fit very well. There were seven little boys and girls and every one of them was dressed in a different color.

"I guess they didn't check their bags," said Honey Bunch soberly. "They must have them on their minds."

Indeed Honey Bunch had never seen so many bags and suitcases and boxes and bundles in one group in all her life. The bundles were so stuffed that they looked as though they might burst open any minute. The suitcases were tied up with ropes and straps and they looked as though they might fall apart if any one tried to unpack the things that were in them.

"Where are they going, Mother?" asked Honey Bunch in a whisper.

"I don't know, dear," Mrs. Morton answered. "They are from some other country and they've come to learn to be Americans. Think of crossing the ocean to

a perfectly strange country and then having
to learn a new language and new ways to do
and live. I wouldn't like to do that, would
you, Honey Bunch?"

"No-o," decided Honey Bunch. "But
what makes them do it, Mother?"

Mrs. Morton explained that the people
probably wanted their children to grow up
in a country where there was more room and
a fairer chance to succeed than in the country
from which they had come.

The seven children stared at Honey Bunch
with solemn dark eyes as she and her mother
walked past them.

"They didn't smile back," complained
Honey Bunch.

Honey Bunch always smiled at every one
and always every one smiled back at her.
It is usually that way, and you may have noticed it; if you're a smiling child, folks smile
at you. But dear me, if you scowl a great
deal, you'll see that nearly every one you
meet scowls, too.

"They're tired and perhaps hungry and

frightened, dear," Mrs. Morton said gently. "They've seen so many strange people and so many strange sights that quite likely they've made up their minds that they do not like this queer America or the strange American people. Wait till they reach their new home, wherever it may be, and settle down and rest; then they'll be cheerful, happy children, we'll hope."

There seemed to be a good many strange looking people—like those they had seen sitting on all their boxes and bundles—and Mrs. Morton explained that Chicago was the point from which many immigrants went to to the Western farms and ranches.

A moment later Mrs. Morton saw a book and magazine stand and she decided that she would get something to read on the train.

"Mother!" whispered Honey Bunch, as they started for the stand where the bright-colored covers of the magazines made the front of the booth look like a picture gallery. "Mother, look! She's crying!"

Sure enough, there was a lady with her

handkerchief up to her eyes and another lady
was patting her on her back.

"Is she sorry?" asked Honey Bunch.
"What makes her cry, Mother?"

"Why, I think some one she loves has gone
off on the train," Mrs. Morton said. "Perhaps some one has gone on a long
journey and she is crying because she knows
how much she will miss the some one. But
when the traveler comes back, Honey Bunch,
think how happy she will feel!"

"Only we won't see her feel happy," suggested Honey Bunch.

"No; but we can imagine how she will
look then," Mrs. Morton said. "In a great
station like this, the happy and the sorry
people meet all the time. See if you can't
find some one who is happy in just a minute."

Honey Bunch held fast to her mother's
hand as they made their way through the
crowd toward the magazine stand, but her
bright eyes watched intently, and in much
less than a minute, Honey Bunch had found
a happy person—three of them, in fact.

"Look, Mother! They're laughing," she whispered.

Three girls were coming toward them, their arms linked together. A porter walked behind them, carrying their suitcases. The girls were all talking at once, and how they did laugh.

"Didn't we have an absolutely perfect time!" said one, as they passed Honey Bunch and her mother.

"They feel happy, don't they?" Honey Bunch said, with much satisfaction. "Are they going away, Mother?"

"I think they have been away and had a lovely time and are glad to be home again," replied Mrs. Morton, smiling.

They had reached the magazines and books by this time and Honey Bunch's mother was much interested in finding a certain magazine that Daddy Morton liked to read. The stand was open on all four sides and Honey Bunch began to walk slowly around it.

She looked at all the pictures and saw one of a farmhouse that looked exactly like the

house in which her Cousin Stub lived. And
there was a picture of a dog that looked almost like Teddy, the brown and white dog
that belonged to Grace Winters.

"I wonder if Grace would like me to bring
her that?" thought Honey Bunch.

She finally decided that if Grace had the
real dog, she didn't need a picture of a dog,
and so she went on to the third side of the
booth.

There she saw something that made her
forget all about the dog picture.

For there were the nicest paper dolls
Honey Bunch had ever seen, all tied in a
box, ready for some little girl to buy. Honey
Bunch was very fond of paper dolls, and she
thought what fun it would be to have some
on the train with her. Eleanor was very nice,
but Eleanor was rather heavy to carry. That
was the reason Daddy Morton had wrapped
her in his coat and checked her with the
bags; he said Eleanor needed a rest and
Honey Bunch did, too.

"I could buy those paper dolls," said

Honey Bunch to herself. "I have lots of money."

She opened her little purse—alas, too quickly!—and one of the bright new pennies jumped out and rolled across the stone floor. It looped and circled and kept rolling and turning, and no one stepped on it, though Honey Bunch expected every minute that a shoe would come down on it.

Honey Bunch couldn't roll through the crowds like the penny, and she had to stop and say "Excuse me" several times and this was the reason she lost track of the circling coin. While she was saying "Excuse me" to an old lady whose knees she had bumped, that penny completely disappeared.

And when Honey Bunch turned around the magazine stand had disappeared too!

CHAPTER VII

MR. BILLY SLADE

HONEY BUNCH was so surprised she stood "stock still," as Mrs. Miller would have said. Mrs. Miller had once told her that stock still was as still as still could be.

"Why—why," said Honey Bunch aloud. "Why—why——"

No one heard her. In that great noisy station a little girl who spoke in an ordinary tone of voice could not be heard at all.

"I know just where that magazine place is," Honey Bunch said, still speaking aloud. "I saw it right over there."

But it wasn't "right over there" at all! Honey Bunch didn't see how anything so large could walk out of the station, but it must have done that, because she couldn't see it in any direction, no matter how hard she looked.

Suddenly it seemed to Honey Bunch that the station was much larger than it had been when she first came into it. Or maybe she was smaller. Yes, that was it—she could feel herself growing smaller. And the station, full of people though it was, seemed very high and very empty. Honey Bunch remembered that Daddy and Mother were going West on the train—they might go without her and there she would be in that great Chicago station without any one to love her, or any place to sleep, or any house of her own to live in!

"Maybe I can find the door," thought Honey Bunch, trying not to cry.

She meant the door where Daddy Morton had said he would meet them.

Honey Bunch started to run. She ran as fast as she could in one direction and only stopped when she found herself up against a wire grating. That wasn't the door she was looking for at all!

Then one tear did brim over, but Honey Bunch winked it away.

"I'm not going to use my new handker-chief," she said firmly. "I—I want to save my new handkerchief."

She felt hot and tired and she would have liked to have sat down for a little rest, only there didn't seem to be any place to sit. Then, far away, she heard some one begin to call out trains and there was no way to find out whether he was calling the train her daddy and mother were planning to take or not.

"I'll ask him," gulped poor little Honey Bunch, and she began to run in the direction of the voice.

But she couldn't find it—in fact, it seemed to her that every step she took the voice sounded still farther away.

Honey Bunch stopped short, wheeled around, and ran straight into a porter who was also running.

"Are you hurt, little girl?" he asked anxiously. "No, I guess you is all right. Look out, I got to make that Number Seven-teen."

He put his head down and began to run
again and he was out of sight before Honey
Bunch could ask him about the door or the
magazine stand, or where to find the train
for the West.

Now Honey Bunch was truly frightened.
She couldn't see a thing in the station that she
had ever noticed before and it seemed to her
that it had all been changed around. Of
course, this was because she was hopelessly
tangled in her directions, and the more she
ran, the more tangled she became.

You might think that people would see a
little girl running to and fro and stop her
and ask if anything was the matter. But
all the people in the station were in a hurry
—they had trains to make or they were worried about getting to a certain place at a certain time. Besides they knew there were
information booths and porters and train men
to help those who wanted help.

Honey Bunch didn't know anything about
the information booths, and if there were any
train men or porters around she didn't see

them—except the one porter who had been too busy to stop a moment. She was only a little lost girl, and she kept hoping every minute to see either Daddy or Mother or the door where Daddy had promised to meet them.

In spite of her determination not to cry, the tears would come into her blue eyes. But she wasn't going to use that pretty new handkerchief—"not to cry on!" said Honey Bunch indignantly—and that was the reason she couldn't see very plainly where she was going.

Her eyes were full of tears when, without warning, she plunged headlong into a young man stooping over an open suitcase on the floor. He grunted, Honey Bunch said "Oh!" and a shaving brush dropped out of his hand and rolled across the floor. At the same time a shower of socks, ties, and clean handkerchiefs seemed to be tumbled out in several directions.

"Say, look here—" began the young man, straightening up.

His voice was gruff and his eyes looked rather angry—until he saw the wet blue ones gazing back at him.

"I'm so sorry!" said Honey Bunch, unconscious that tears were rolling down her cheeks. "I fell over you."

"I had no business to be taking up so much space," the young man declared. "It's all my fault for being so careless. Did you hurt yourself?"

Honey Bunch shook her head.

"I'm all right," she said bravely, "only—I lost myself. I can't find my m-mother."

"You poor kid!" the young man exclaimed, and now his voice wasn't a bit gruff and his eyes were very kind. "Don't you care! We'll find Mother for you."

He reached for one of the tumbled handkerchiefs and very gently wiped Honey Bunch's brimming eyes.

"Don't you care," he repeated, patting her on the back. "You're not really lost, you know."

Honey Bunch felt better at once. She supposed it was because some one had patted her on the back when she cried.

The young man put his handkerchief in his pocket and looked gravely at Honey Bunch.

"I think I'd better get my stuff together and then see what is to be done—don't you?" he suggested.

Honey Bunch nodded.

"I'll help you," she said, beginning to fold the handkerchiefs and socks neatly.

She didn't offer to go after the shaving brush—why, if she went to pick that up, for all she knew when she turned around the young man and his suitcase might have disappeared! Honey Bunch had had enough of running after rolling things to last her a long, long time.

Together she and the young man got that suitcase into order. He told her that he had been repacking it when she fell over him.

"I'm a careless kind of individual," the young man said, "and I throw my stuff in as long as I can close the lid; when I can't shut

the suitcase, I know the time has come to do
a little real packing."

At last all the scattered articles were col-
lected and everything was neatly arranged
and the suitcase closed with the two straps
buckled around it.

"And now, we go and find your mother,"
said the young man.

"And my daddy," Honey Bunch added.
The young man put his hands in his
pockets and looked down at her.

"Have you lost your whole family?" he
asked, his eyes twinkling.

Honey Bunch did not feel frightened any
more. She was sure that this tall, thin person—she told Mother afterward that when
he was folded up he wasn't so tall, but when
he stood up he was taller than Daddy—
would find her mother and daddy for her
without a bit of trouble.

"We're going West," Honey Bunch Morton informed her new friend.

"West?" he said instantly. "How far West
are you going?"

Honey Bunch didn't know. Worse still, she couldn't remember the name of the ranch or any of the stations Daddy had read to her. She was still excited and tired from running about the big station and she couldn't think quickly.

"Never mind—we'll manage," the young man said cheerfully. "You might tell me your name—that will help."

"I'm Honey Bunch Morton," explained Honey Bunch. "My real name is Gertrude Marion Morton. And my daddy is Mr. Morton."

"Yes'm," the young man said. "And I'm very glad to know you, Miss Honey Bunch. My name is Billy Slade."

"We live in Barham," announced Honey Bunch. "Where do you live?"

"Oh, I travel around," Mr. Billy Slade said, not quite so cheerfully. "But I'm a Westerner by birth. You could see the Rocky Mountains from the window of my house."

Honey Bunch slipped her hand into his.

"Let's go find Mother," she urged happily.

She liked Mr. Billy Slade. She liked him very much. She liked his voice, even when it had been gruff, and she liked the way he smiled down at her and she liked the way he lifted the heavy suitcase as though he found it easy to carry.

"I wish," said Honey Bunch, as they waited a moment, "you were going West with us."

Mr. Billy Slade smiled—his face was so tanned that when he smiled his teeth looked very white—and then he put down the suitcase.

"I want you to try to think, Honey Bunch," he said slowly. "Try hard to think of where you are going. Don't you see, if I know where you are going, I can find out where the train is, the track it will be on, I mean, and your daddy and mother will be there."

Honey Bunch thought so hard a little wrinkle grew between her eyes.

"I know," she said at length. "It is the

three-forty-five train—Daddy said so Is
that all right?"

Mr. Billy Slade laughed, becau e he
couldn't help it. He said that it was better
than nothing, but if more than one tı ⎜ın left
at 3:45—as was likely—they might have a
little trouble finding the right one.

"However, we won't cross bridges before
we come to them," he declared. "Forward—
march, Honey Bunch."

He took her hand again and lifted his
suitcase and they started off.

"Carry your bag, sir?" called a porter,
hurrying up to them.

"No; I'll take it. But I want you to do
something else," said Mr. Billy Slade
quickly. "This little girl has become sep-
arated from her mother and father. I'd like
you and two or three others to go through
the crowds calling out his name. Morton is
the name. You get a couple of your buddies
and call for Mr. Morton. Ten chances to one
either he or Mrs. Morton is milling about on
the main floor, searching for the little girl."

"Yes, sir," said the porter, scratching his head. "All right sir. But where do we find you after we find Mr. Morton?"

"We'll be down on the train levels, some-where," Mr. Billy Slade answered. "The Mortons are taking the three-forty-five west and I've got to find out what track it's on. You tell Mr. Morton he'll find us at the train gate—he'll know which level it is." Then he told the porter his name so the man could tell it to Mr. Morton.

"You ain't got much time," said the porter, scratching his head again.

"Well, I know it," Mr. Billy Slade said, using his gruff voice. "I've got to do the best I can! See that you do the same."

Honey Bunch saw him give the porter some money and the man hurried away.

CHAPTER VIII

HONEY BUNCH IS FOUND

Mr. Billy Slade walked so fast that Honey Bunch had to take little running steps in order to keep up with him. He smiled down at her every now and then, though most of the time his eyes were searching the crowds anxiously.

"That man said 'ain't got'," said Honey Bunch, panting a little as she tried to talk and run at the same time.

"Grammar," replied Mr. Billy Slade seriously, "is important. But you know how it is—when folks get excited, they forget their learning."

"Oh, yes, I know how it is!" Honey Bunch agreed. "I forget my learning, too. I wish I could think of where we are going."

Then suddenly she saw a crowd of people and Mr. Billy Slade saw them, too.

"When you see a mob like that," he told
her, "you can be sure you are coming to the information booth. I never saw anything like
the way some people yearn to be informed."

"Are they all going somewhere?" asked
Honey Bunch, staring doubtfully at the
crowd.

"They think they are," Mr. Billy Slade
said, and his gruff voice had come back. "I
haven't any time to waste, and I suppose I'll
have to stand in line."

Honey Bunch had the brightest eyes in the
world—her daddy often said so—and she saw
at once that there were several lines of people
standing at the information booth.

"Maybe you can find a short line," suggested Honey Bunch. She had noticed that
there were more people in some of the lines
than in others.

"That's a good idea," Mr. Billy Slade re-
turned, with approval. "This looks as short
as any of 'em. Here, Honey Bunch, you sit
on my suitcase and don't you stir, no matter
if the roof falls on you!"

"Oh, I won't stir," promised Honey Bunch
in her clear little voice. "I won't stir a single
stir! I would hate to get lost again."

She sat very quietly on the suitcase and
watched Mr. Billy Slade's broad back as he
stood in line. Every time some one finished
talking to the clerk and stepped away, the
line moved a little. But it was pretty slow
waiting and some of the people must have
asked a thousand questions, Honey Bunch
thought.

When she finally saw Mr. Billy Slade
reach the desk, she gave a little sigh of relief.
She saw him turn and point to her and the
clerk put his glasses up on his forehead and
looked at her. Honey Bunch didn't mind—
she knew that Mr. Billy Slade must be telling
the clerk about her and asking him about the
trains.

It took Mr. Billy Slade quite as long as any
of the others who had stood in line to find
out what he wanted, but when he came back
to Honey Bunch he was smiling.

"We're making progress," he told her.

"There are four trains leaving here at three-forty-five, but only two of them are for points west, so that simplifies matters. Now if we can get settled which is your train, we are fixed. The two tracks are rather far apart, so it's necessary to be careful in our choice."

Honey Bunch looked anxiously at him.

"How can we tell?" she asked.

"We have to trust to luck," said Mr. Billy Slade. "The clerk told me, Honey Bunch, that one of these trains makes most of its stops at large cities. It's almost a through train to the coast, in fact. Do you think you're going to a big city, or perhaps out to California?"

"Oh, no!" exclaimed Honey Bunch, glad that she could answer this question. "We're not going to California. We're going to a ranch! It wasn't on the map, but funny places like Deadwood were. Only we aren't going to Deadwood."

But Mr. Billy Slade seemed to be pleased. "You and I," he declared, "are heading

for track thirty-seven. That's the train that
goes to the end of nowhere. The clerk told
me."

"I don't think we're going to the end of nowhere, either," objected Honey Bunch.

"Well, perhaps the station you want comes
before that," Mr. Billy Slade said, laughing.

Honey Bunch was sure that this Chicago
station must be the largest in the world. She
had walked—she thought—miles and miles,
hunting for her daddy and mother, not to
mention the long walk she and Mother had
taken together before Honey Bunch was
lost.

Then she and Mr. Billy Slade had walked
and walked, and now, to reach Track 37, it
seemed they must walk more and walk faster,
too.

"I'll bet you're tired out," said Mr. Billy
Slade suddenly. "Want me to carry you,
Honey Bunch?"

"I'd rather walk," Honey Bunch answered
truthfully. "But could I have a drink of
water?"

Mr. Billy Slade glanced at the station clock, then saw a drinking fountain close at hand.

"All right," he said. "I wouldn't drag you around like this, Honey Bunch, but I can guess how important it is for your dad to get that train."

He put down the suitcase, for the faucet was too high for Honey Bunch to reach. There was a glass case filled with paper drinking cups and he felt in his pocket to get a penny for the slot. You had to put a penny in, before you could get a cup.

"Well—" he said a little jerkily, and Honey Bunch saw with surprise that his face was turning red under the tan. "What do you know about that! I don't seem to have a penny."

"I have!" cried Honey Bunch eagerly. "I have ten—no, one rolled out of my purse. But I have dozens of pennies! Wait a minute."

She hastily opened her pretty blue purse and took out one of the bright new pennies.

"Aren't you saving that?" asked Mr. Billy Slade.

"They're to buy things with," Honey Bunch assured him. "Daddy said so."

Then Mr. Billy Slade put the cent in the slot of the glass case and turned the crank and out came a nice little white cup.

He filled it with the ice-cold water and gave it to Honey Bunch, who was sure she had never been half as thirsty before as she was at that moment. She drank two cups of water and then Mr. Billy Slade said he didn't believe she ought to drink any more. Not just then.

"You get one," said Honey Bunch, holding out a penny to him on the palm of her hand.

He had tossed away her cup and she knew that only one person was supposed to drink out of a cup—that was why they had them in a stack in a glass case.

The tall young man bent down and gently closed the four little fingers and thumb across the penny.

"I'm not thirsty," he said, "and we must

hurry. There isn't a great deal of time to lose, Honey Bunch."

Honey Bunch put the penny back in her purse and slipped her hand into Mr. Billy Slade's. He lifted the heavy suitcase and they began to walk as fast as they could again.

Honey Bunch had a clear little brain and there was very little she did not see, though she did not always understand all she saw. Now she was wondering about Mr. Billy Slade, who had no pennies in his pocket.

"He gave the porter man some money to go and call out Daddy's name," she thought. "He gave him quite a lot of money—I heard it rattle. Maybe he gave him all the money he had and now he hasn't any."

Then Honey Bunch began to remember other things. She remembered that while the suitcase—Mr. Billy Slade's suitcase— was heavy and bulky, there really wasn't a great deal in it. When she and Mr. Billy Slade had everything all folded up and in its right place, the suitcase had not been more than half full. And there was a patch right on top of his shoe! She had not seen it till now, but walking beside him, she could see his tan shoes very plainly. There was a large patch on the side of one of them.

However, Mr. Billy Slade wasn't worrying about patches on his shoes or lack of pennies in his pocket. All he thought about was find-ing Track 37, and when he and Honey Bunch finally found themselves in a grim gray kind of place, with iron gates and rows of railroad tracks and a general air of coal dust and smoke settling on the windows and the cars standing still on the tracks, he ac-tually began to hum a little tune.

"Watch the number, Honey Bunch," he said cheerfully. "See those big black and white numbers? We want a three and a seven."

But Honey Bunch didn't have to watch the numbers, after all. Some distance away she saw a man in a blue uniform standing be-hind an iron railing at one of the gates. A crowd of people were before this railing, most of them with bags in their hands or at

their feet. More people and porters with
baggage kept coming. Honey Bunch was
wondering whether this could possibly be
Track 37 when she saw some one, all in gray
and with a bunch of violets in her hat, break
away from the crowd and coming running
toward her.

"There's Mother!" cried Honey Bunch,
dropping Mr. Billy Slade's hand and rushing
ahead. "Oh, Mother, did you miss me?"

Well, Daddy Morton was right there, too,
and if Honey Bunch didn't use her best blue
handkerchief when she cried, she was perfectly willing to lend it to her mother. For
Mrs. Morton cried—just a little—and then
she smiled, and when she smiled at Mr. Billy
Slade that young man looked as though he
might need a blue handkerchief himself in
just a minute.

"The gate isn't open yet—come over here
and let's get straightened out," said Mr. Morton, leading them to one side where they
would not be in the way of the people hurrying to find their trains.

"Was that your idea to send a porter to page Mr. Morton?" asked Honey Bunch's mother, looking at Mr. Billy Slade. "It was very clever and I think the only way we should have found each other in time to make the train. As soon as the man found us— we were asking every one we met if they had seen a little girl alone—he told us you would met us at the train gate."

"I didn't think Honey Bunch would remember the train, but I knew you must have found out in some way," Mr. Morton said. "If we had missed this train I should have been in a fine mess."

"Well, I'm glad it's all right, and now I'd better be on my way," said Mr. Billy Slade a little awkwardly.

Mr. Morton smiled and glanced at his wife.

"Finding our little girl and bringing her back to us isn't exactly a casual performance," he remarked. "You're going to let Honey Bunch's father put his gratitude into something a little more substantial than words, I hope."

Honey Bunch, listening, wasn't quite sure
what Daddy meant. But she recognized Mr.
Billy Slade's gruff voice when he spoke.

"I don't want anything," said Mr. Billy
Slade almost rudely. "And what's more, I
won't take anything."

But he didn't know Honey Bunch's daddy,
if he thought that settled it.

"Edith, you and Honey Bunch will have
to take care of each other for a few minutes,"
said Mr. Morton. "I want a word or two
with this obstinate young man—yes, sweet-
heart, what is it?"

Honey Bunch drew his head down to her
lips.

"Daddy, he hasn't any pennies," she whispered in his ear.

"I'll be back directly," said Mr. Morton
calmly. "Leave your suitcase, Slade. We'll
just take a turn or two down the platform."

CHAPTER IX

HEADING WEST

HONEY BUNCH and her mother took care of their two bags and Mr. Billy Slade's suitcase until Mr. Morton and the young Westerner came back. They were gone longer than a few minutes, and in the mean time the iron gate had opened and all the people waiting for the train had shown their tickets and gone through.

"It would be dreadful if we should miss the train after all," said Mrs. Morton nervously.

"Here comes Daddy!" cried Honey Bunch joyfully.

Mr. Billy Slade was smiling now, and he had lost his gruff voice once more. But when he saw that the crowd was gone, he seemed anxious.

"Is it train time?" he asked worriedly.

"We'll make it," Mr. Morton said confidently. "Say good-by, Honey Bunch, and ask Mr. Slade to come to see us in Barham."

"Please come and see us in Barham, Mr. Billy Slade," said Honey Bunch eagerly. "And thank you ever so much for finding me."

Then she stood on tiptoe to kiss Mr. Billy Slade, who seemed to like that amazingly.

"You're the nicest little girl I ever knew in all my life," he said earnestly.

Then Honey Bunch's mother shook hands with him and asked him to *please* come and see them if he ever had a chance, and Honey Bunch's daddy shook hands with him and wished him "the best of luck." Then a man inside the gate shouted something and Mr. Billy Slade exclaimed. "Good grief, you'll have to run for it!"

A porter came from somewhere and took their bags, Mr. Morton took Honey Bunch by one hand and put his other hand under his wife's elbow, and the three of them did "run for it."

Honey Bunch looked once and saw Mr. Billy Slade, who took off his hat and waved it at her.

"Eleanor!" gasped the breathless Honey Bunch, as she was lifted up the car steps. "Where's Eleanor?"

"She's perfectly safe, dear," Mrs. Morton answered. "Daddy's coat has been around her every minute. Won't it seem fine to get settled in our own compartment and know that for the next few hours we won't have to do any hurrying?"

Honey Bunch was staring at the car in astonishment. She had never seen a car like this. There was a row of doors and they apparently opened into rooms—and whoever heard of rooms on a train?

"Those are the compartments, Honey Bunch," her mother said. "In this car there are fourteen of them. There's the porter beckoning to us—he has found ours."

When Honey Bunch followed her mother into the compartment, she was more surprised than ever.

"It's a regular house, isn't it, Mother?" she exclaimed as the door closed behind the porter who went out. "A regular house, but all in one room."

Well, so it was—that is, it was almost like a regular house. There was a wide window and pleasant seats—by and by these would mysteriously be made into a bed, said Mrs. Morton. There was a full length mirror set in the door and a little dressing room attached with a basin almost like the one in the bathroom at home.

"I'm so glad Honey Bunch and I won't have to walk down to the other end of the car and take our turn when we want to wash our faces in the morning," said Mrs. Morton. "We can be by ourselves here, and do exactly as we please."

"Yes, and if you like, we can eat in here." Honey Bunch's daddy declared. "You might like breakfast served that way, but I think Honey Bunch will get more fun out of the dining car."

"Honey Bunch looks as though she was

having a very good time this minute," said
Mrs. Morton, smiling.

Honey Bunch smiled, too. She had ex-
plored every corner of the compartment and
she had unwrapped Eleanor and straightened
her crumpled cloak. Now the doll was sitting next to the window and Honey Bunch
climbed up on the seat beside her.

"Tell about Mr. Billy Slade, please,
Daddy—Oh!" she said.

She said "Oh," because the train had been
moving so slowly and quietly that she had
hardly realized they were going. Now it
had left the long gray shed and the burst of
sunshine was startling.

"Yes, Daddy, do tell us about Mr. Billy
Slade," urged Mrs. Morton, seating herself
opposite to Honey Bunch. "Tell us what he
said and what you said."

Mr. Morton laughed. He had taken off
his hat and stowed the bags out of the way,
and now he looked as though, like Honey
Bunch, he was ready to enjoy every minute
of the trip.

"I thought at first that Mr. Billy Slade wasn't going to say anything," he confessed. "I imagine he can be a remarkably silent young man when he chooses to be. However, I got him to tell me how he found Honey Bunch and by a little angling I forced him to admit that he has been a little down on his luck. I noticed that his shoes were patched and he looked a little thinner, I thought, than even an active young chap ought to be."

"He didn't have any pennies," murmured Honey Bunch.

"I was glad you mentioned that," said her daddy. "It gave me an opening. I asked him pointblank if he had tipped the porter, and he admitted that he had. I asked him if he had tipped the man with his last bit of change, and he had to admit that, too. So then I asked him what he did for a living and what his immediate plans were and he told me, grudgingly at first, a little more graciously, as I led him on."

"He looks like an outdoor man," said Mrs. Morton.

"He is," said her husband. "He has worked on ranches all his life, he told me. It seems that he has held a fairly good position for the last year, but the ranch changed ownership and a new foreman came in. Slade couldn't hit it off with the fellow and left. Unfortunately, his married sister had to have help—her husband and children were sick and one of the children had to have an expensive operation—and he turned over all his savings to her. His theory is that a man can always get some kind of work, but he was down to his last twenty dollars when he got the offer of a job as foreman on some ranch."

"Will he like it?" asked Honey Bunch anxiously.

"He's keen about it," Mr. Morton replied, "because it is his first job as foreman. They've advanced him his railroad fare, but most of his twenty went for clothing he had to have and I got out of him that he would arrive at the ranch without a cent in his pocket. The little change he had when he met Honey Bunch, he handed to the porter."

"Oh, David, I hope you made him accept some money!" said Mrs. Morton. "Why, he may have to work a month without any money."

"Exactly what I pointed out to him," Honey Bunch's daddy replied. "I finally got him to take a loan—he flatly refused to consider it a gift—of thirty dollars. I held out for fifty, but we had to compromise. Anyway, he's young and healthy and has a job. Thirty dollars will help him over a rough spot or two, perhaps, and certainly get him a pair of shoes."

Then Honey Bunch told Daddy and Mother what had happened to her and how she lost the magazine stand, and her mother told Honey Bunch how, when she had missed her, she had hunted up and down the station for her and then, at last, when she couldn't find her, had gone back to the door, where Daddy Morton had found her almost crying.

"Then we both began to hunt for you and when we heard the porter calling, 'Mr. Mor-

ton—Mr. Morton—Mr. Morton,' we knew
that he must be bringing us news about our
little girl," said Mrs. Morton.

Honey Bunch explained that she had forgotten the name of the ranch and that Mr.
Billy Slade said you forgot your learning
when you were excited.

"I couldn't remember the name of the station where we are going, either," said Honey
Bunch.

"Heart of gold, you never heard it," her
daddy told her. "The ranch is Three Rock
Ranch—yes, now you remember that. But
the station is a little speck called Thompsontown. I doubt if it is on any map."

Honey Bunch was sure that no one had
ever told her they were going to Thompsontown. She would, she said, remember a name
like that.

"Then come along and test your excellent
memory on the diner," said her daddy, leaning over to tickle her under her chin. "See
if you can remember your daddy's favorite
dessert, Honey Bunch."

"Charlotte russe!" Honey Bunch giggled.

"Now, David," said Mrs. Morton, "I am surprised at you! In the first place, it can't be anywhere near time to eat. In the second place, how can you even think of charlotte russe when you and Honey Bunch had such enormous ones for your luncheon?"

"Honey Bunch and I have healthy appetites," her husband answered. "I really feel a little faint, Mother. Don't you think I ought to have an early dinner when I feel a little faint?"

Mrs. Morton laughed and said that she supposed they might as well go into the dining car. But, she added, no one should think of eating charlotte russe more than once a day.

Honey Bunch washed her face and hands at the cunning little wash basin and dried them with a blue-bordered towel. Then she brushed her yellow hair and put on a yellow pongee frock, because her mother said that while dark clothes were sensible to travel in, she did like to see her little girl in a clean bright frock, the kind of dress she would wear at home.

"Isn't it nice to eat on the train!" said Honey Bunch, smiling so cheerfully at the few early diners in the car that every one of them smiled back at her.

There was a very sober-faced waiter at their table, but, my goodness, how he did beam when he lifted Honey Bunch into her chair. He even went and found a cushion for her to sit on because the chair wasn't high enough.

"To-morrow morning I'll have some blocks to go under your chair," he told her. "I got my mind's eye on some blocks that will make it just right for you."

Honey Bunch was interested in hearing more about his mind's eye, but as her daddy was studying the menu card and asking her mother what she would like for dinner, Honey Bunch wisely decided that perhaps the waiter would be too busy to answer many questions.

"They have very good sounding desserts

Mother," said Mr. Morton, a twinkle in his eye. "Do you suppose they taste as good as they sound?"

"No one has any dessert who doesn't eat a sensible dinner first," Mrs. Morton reminded him. "Soup and baked potato and spinach and a chop. Then we'll see about the dessert."

Now Honey Bunch was really hungry and so was her daddy, and they ate the delicious and sensible dinner Mrs. Morton ordered, not only to please her, but to please themselves. More people came into the dining car as they were eating and Honey Bunch was delighted when she saw a little girl about her own age eating at a table farther down the car.

"There's a little girl, Mother," she announced, "and a little boy. Would it be all right to go and speak to them?"

"Well, I wouldn't to-night," said her mother. "If they have had as exciting a day as you have, I think they will want to go to bed early and go to sleep, so as to be ready to make new friends to-morrow."

Honey Bunch thought to-morrow would be a nice day to make new friends, and when she and her daddy had had vanilla ice-cream —ice-cream always reminded Honey Bunch of a party—they were ready to go back to the compartment.

Passing through the car ahead of the diner, Honey Bunch stooped suddenly and picked up something from the carpet.

"It must belong to the waiter," she said when her mother asked her what she had found. "I think it's his mind's eye!"

CHAPTER X

DETECTIVE WORK

MRS. MORTON looked puzzled and the people sitting near by laughed. Mr. Morton had not heard what Honey Bunch said, but when they reached their compartment and Mrs. Morton told him and Honey Bunch showed him the "mind's eye," he laughed so much that Honey Bunch was really alarmed.

"David, for pity's sake! Oh, David, people will think you've lost your mind," said Mrs. Morton, beginning to laugh, too, as Honey Bunch's daddy put his head down on his arms and laughed and laughed.

Presently Honey Bunch began to laugh, too, though she couldn't see any joke.

"What is funny?" she kept asking. "Daddy, what is funny?"

"You are, Honey Bunch," he said, sitting up straight and wiping his eyes. "Let's see this mind's eye you were talking about."

He looked as though he might be about to laugh again, but he didn't. Honey Bunch had shown him what she had found when they first came back, but he had laughed so much he had not had a good look at it.

"That's the eye out of some toy animal, dear," he explained now. "You remember the cat Grandma Elder showed you on the train? Didn't it have eyes something like this?"

"Yes, it did," nodded Honey Bunch. "I remember. But where is the toy cat?"

"We'll have to do a little detective work," Mr. Morton declared. "You and I, Honey Bunch, will look at every toy cat we meet and the first one we see that has only one eye we'll say 'A-ha! So you're the cat who lost her eye!'"

Honey Bunch rather wanted to start out right away and hunt for a toy cat with one eye gone, but her mother said that good detectives should go to bed early and start their work in the morning.

"Mrs. Miller does her best work in the

morning, so perhaps we'd better go to bed early," said Honey Bunch.

Her daddy thought that was a good plan and he went off to the smoking car—and to tell the waiter, Honey Bunch rather suspected, about the mind's eye; that is, if he should happen to meet the waiter. Daddy Morton just loved to tell jokes.

The porter came in to make up the beds and this interested Honey Bunch very much. There was a bed as long as her mother's bed at home and almost as wide, and a smaller bed just right for a little girl like Honey Bunch. Whoever had invented them, Honey Bunch confided to Mother, must have been a good inventor, because in the daytime you couldn't tell there was a bed anywhere in the room.

"When Norman Clark's mother went to California," said Honey Bunch, cuddling down cozily in her little bed, "she slept behind curtains. And you had to dress and undress where the curtains were, Mother, so people couldn't see you."

"Well, Mrs. Clark went in a sleeping car,"
Mrs. Morton explained. "I have slept in
that kind of a car, too. The beds are called
berths and they are on both sides of the car,
in a double row. Curtains let down so that
the people asleep and getting ready to sleep
or getting up in the morning, can not be seen.
Daddy was good to get on a compartment
car, because it is so much more convenient."

"Almost," murmured Honey Bunch
sleepily, "almost—like—almost—like—the
stateroom—on the—Bermuda ship."

She was fast asleep in two minutes, and
though she woke up once during the night
and heard the wheels of the train singing
a little song as they rolled along, she could
not stay awake long enough to find out what
the wheels were saying.

"I'll ask Daddy in the morning," she
thought, and the next time she opened her
eyes and heard the wheels singing it *was*
morning.

Honey Bunch sat up in bed and saw her
mother brushing her hair.

"Hello, little sleepy head!" said Mother. "Daddy is shaving—he'll be through in a moment. How did you sleep during your first night on a train?"

"It was fun," Honey Bunch answered. "I have to do detective work to-day, Mother, don't I?"

Mrs. Morton had forgotten about the cat's eye, but now she remembered. She said she would help Honey Bunch dress quickly, so they could have breakfast, and then she and her daddy could begin their detective work.

"I have to ask Daddy something else," murmured Honey Bunch, but there was so much to do to get ready for breakfast that Honey Bunch had to wait till they were seated at their table in the dining car before she could ask her daddy what it was the train wheels kept singing.

The colored waiter smiled at her so broadly that Honey Bunch was quite sure he had heard about the mistake she had made—but Honey Bunch never minded how much people laughed. Usually she laughed back at them, no matter if the joke was about her.

"Daddy," she said, as she began to eat her cereal, "what do the wheels say? Listen— hear them singing?"

Daddy and Mother both listened and both said they could hear a song.

"Why, I think I can make out the words," declared Daddy Morton. "Let me listen again—yes, sir, I can hear it very distinctly."

Honey Bunch's eyes began to dance.

"Sing it, Daddy!" she urged. "Please sing it."

"Mother, may I sing at the table?" Mr. Morton asked. "Just this once, Mother? Please?"

Mrs. Morton laughed.

"I suppose, as this is a very special occasion, you will have to sing at the table," she admitted.

Just then some more people came into the diner and Honey Bunch, glancing across to the next table, saw the little boy and girl she had noticed the night before. Only then they had sat farther away.

"My daddy is going to sing what the wheels sing," said Honey Bunch, with her friendly smile.

The little boy and girl stared. They seemed to be delighted. Mr. Morton made them a little bow and then he sang. He sang in a low tone so that only those at the two tables could hear him.

"Click-clack! Do your best! Honey Bunch is going West!" sang Mr. Morton. "Click-clack! Clear the track! Soon she will be coming back!"

Honey Bunch nodded her yellow head in delight.

"That's *exactly* what the wheels sing!" she cried. "Isn't it?" she asked, turning to the little girl at the next table.

"Yes, it is," agreed the little girl, while her mother smiled. "I never knew before what the wheels say as they turn, but that is just like it."

All the children wanted to sing the song then and there, but the two mothers said they thought that one song was enough, so instead

they became acquainted with each other,
which was just as nice.

Honey Bunch told them who she was and
where she lived and where she was going.
They told her that they were Gwen and
Peter March and that they lived in New
York and were going to a place called Gopher, which they would reach early the next
morning.

"I have a doll, Eleanor," said Honey
Bunch, when she had finished her breakfast.
"Don't you want to come and see her?"

"Gwen has a make-believe dog," Peter
said. "We can bring that to see your
doll."

Gwen and Peter had not yet finished eating,
so the Mortons told them in which car they
were and how to find the compartment and
went away.

Honey Bunch brushed Eleanor's hair and
pulled up her socks and made her all ready
for company. But when, twenty minutes
later, a knock sounded on the door, only Peter
stood there when Mrs. Morton opened it.

"I came to tell you that Gwen can't come,"
said Peter sadly. "She's crying her eyes out,
because she just found that Ming Toy has
lost his left eye. Mother says she can get him
another, but Gwen won't stop crying."

"Who is Ming Toy?" asked Honey Bunch's
mother sympathetically.

"He's Gwen's toy dog," Peter explained.
"She makes an awful fuss over him."

"Oh, Peter!" cried Honey Bunch. "I
found the eye! Didn't I, Mother? I found
it on the floor of the car next to the diner
last night. I—I thought it was something
else at first" (Honey Bunch blushed a rosy
pink) "but Daddy said it was an eye from
some toy animal. We thought maybe it was
a cat."

Daddy Morton was reading by the window, but he had overheard and he took the
glass eye out of his pocket and gave it to
Honey Bunch.

"Is this Ming Toy's eye?" she asked Peter
eagerly.

"Yes, it is," said Peter. "At least it looks

just like his other eye. Gwen will know as
soon as she sees it."

"Ask her to come and bring the dog with
her and I'll glue in the eye," Mrs. Morton
promised. "We have liquid glue in one of
the bags. Daddy, will you find it like a
dear?"

Peter hurrried off to get Gwen, and Honey
Bunch and her daddy decided that it must be
very easy work to be a detective. Mrs. Morton glued the eye in the brown and white toy
dog Gwen presently brought with her, and the
rest of the morning the three children played
together happily, for when they were tired
of Eleanor and Ming Toy, Peter brought out
a new game some one had given him.

They had lunch together in the dining car
and went out on the observation platform
with Mr. Morton, while the two mothers had
a little visit together.

The platform was like a porch, with a
heavy high rail to keep passengers from falling off. There were wicker chairs, like porch
furniture, and Mr. Morton sat down in one

of these and took Honey Bunch on his lap.
Gwen and Peter sat in two other chairs, close
by.

"Daddy!" cried Honey Bunch, staring in
tently into the distance. "Daddy, look!"

She pointed down the track, for the observation car was the last car of the train and
from its platform you could see miles and
miles of country.

"The tracks come together," said Honey
Bunch. "They make a point. Is that where
the tracks start, Daddy?"

"No, it isn't, is it, Mr. Morton?" Peter
chimed in. "The tracks started in Chicago.
That wasn't a point."

Honey Bunch remembered the rows of
tracks in the train shed at Chicago. The
tracks had not run into points there.

"But these do come together," she insisted.

"That is only because of the way we're
looking at them," said Mr. Morton quietly.
"You'll find that two straight lines always
seem to come together in the distance, though
they really do not. If the train should start

and run backward, you'd find the rails would look as though they were coming to a point in the other direction."

Gwen said she didn't see why they looked that way and Mr. Morton told her it was one of the things that she would understand when she was older.

"But, Daddy, the scenery is falling behind," Honey Bunch declared. "I can see it fall."

Gwen declared that she could see the scenery falling, too.

"It *drops*," she insisted.

"Well, the same explanation will have to do for that," said Mr. Morton, smiling. "The scenery only looks as though it is falling behind the train. Your eyes, Honey Bunch—and yours, Gwen—play you tricks."

CHAPTER XI

THE LAST DAY

THE rest of the time Gwen and Peter spent on the train, they were out on the observation platform as much as they were allowed, watching the tracks "make a point," as Gwen called it.

Honey Bunch liked to watch the tracks, too, but the next day, when Gwen and Peter got off the train with their mother at Gopher, Honey Bunch was so lonely she said she didn't know what to do.

Gwen and Peter left the train before breakfast—they had said good-by to Honey Bunch the night before—but Daddy Morton had promised to call her, and he did. He and she were up and dressed, and though the train reached the Gopher station at quarter to seven, Honey Bunch was ready to wave to Gwen and Peter and Mrs. March as they stood on the platform with their baggage around them.

"Gwen will have a little girl to play with," said Honey Bunch to her daddy. "She told me about her. Her name is Alice and she lives next door to the cousin Gwen is going to visit. But I haven't any one to play with now."

"You have me," her daddy reminded her. "And to-morrow you will be getting off the train yourself, and that will be exciting, as you call it."

That morning Honey Bunch and her daddy had breakfast in the dining car together (the waiter had got the little blocks of wood to put under Honey Bunch's chair by this time, and it was just the right height), but Mrs. Morton had her coffee and toast on a table the porter carried to the compartment. She had a slight headache and she told Honey Bunch that she would like to rest as much as she could that day.

"Because after we get to Thompsontown, we have still more traveling to do," she explained, "and of course I want to be able to enjoy our first glimpse of the new places."

So Honey Bunch and her daddy stayed out on the observation platform while Mrs. Morton had an after-breakfast nap. The train stopped at a little station just before noon and many of the passengers got out and walked on the platform. My goodness, you don't know how delightful that seemed—just to walk up and down on the platform boards for seven or eight minutes!

"I like it on a train," said Honey Bunch earnestly, "but I like it on the ground, too."

There was nothing to see at the station but a little waiting room and a great water tank, for the engines took on water here.

"Not even a magazine stand," grumbled one of the passengers.

But Honey Bunch didn't grumble. She thought of the big Chicago station and of all her troubles in that busy place, and she decided that small stations were better, after all.

"Where did Mr. Billy Slade go, Daddy?"

she asked, as the order came for them all to
go back into the train.

"Somewhere out in this direction, I believe," Mr. Morton answered. "I'm not sure
it was as far west as we're going. But it was
a ranch, and from what I could make out, in
the cattle country. He half promised to let
me hear from him as soon as he was settled
in his new job, but I don't think he finds it
very easy to write letters. I don't expect to
hear from him."

Mrs. Morton was still asleep, so they had
lunch and then Mr. Morton read to Honey
Bunch till she, too, fell asleep, and when she
woke up, her mother was awake and reading
the paper. She said her headache was all
gone and that she and Honey Bunch must
write their post-cards, if they were ever going
to.

"The porter will mail them for us and the
children will like to have a post-card mailed
while you are still on the train," said Mrs.
Morton.

Honey Bunch thought this was fun, too,

and her mother wrote with her fountain pen
exactly what Honey Bunch asked her to.
They had bought the cards in Chicago and
Honey Bunch was only sorry that she could
not send one to Mr Billy Slade.

However, she sent cards to Ida Camp, to
Kitty and Cora Williams, to Anna Martin.
She sent one to Grace Winters with a line to
tell her to let her dog Teddy know that a
girl on the train had a toy dog that looked
like him. Cards for Mary and Fannie Graham came next.

Then Honey Bunch remembered Elmer
Gray and his brother, Teddy, and Albert
Barnes. And of course she sent a post card to
Mrs. Miller and asked her to give Honey
Bunch's love to Lady Clare.

"I don't know what to tell Norman Clark,"
sighed Honey Bunch, when all the other
cards had been written and she herself had
pasted on the stamps very neatly. "Would
you tell him I don't think I can get him a
pistol, Mother?"

"No, I don't think I should tell him that,"

Mrs. Morton said. "I wouldn't mention a pistol, if I were you."

"Tell him we're going to have charlotte russe for dessert," Mr. Morton suggested.

"Oh-h, are we?" beamed Honey Bunch. "Mother, are we going to have charlotte russe for dessert?"

"I shouldn't wonder," Mrs. Morton admitted. "This is our last night on the train and I suppose you and Daddy will have to celebrate."

So that was written on Norman's card and the porter promised to mail them at the next station. Honey Bunch and her daddy had so much fun at dinner that night that Mrs. Morton said she didn't know what the waiter would think of them. What he really did think of them was shown when he brought the dessert. He had piled so much charlotte russe on the plate he intended for Honey Bunch, that even her daddy laughed when he saw it.

"My stars, Moses, no child can eat that amount of whipped cream," he protested.

"Why, you must have been bribing the cook!"

"No, sir, I just thought a nice little girl like that ought to have plenty to eat," said the waiter, looking disappointed.

But he was very nice about it and when he had brought two extra plates and Mrs. Morton had divided the charlotte and showed him that there was enough for all three, he admitted that perhaps too much dessert would not be good for Honey Bunch.

The Mortons went to bed early that night, for Mr. Morton said they had a busy day ahead of them. Honey Bunch could go to sleep now singing the words the wheels sang —"Click-clack! Do your best! Honey Bunch is going West. Click-clack! Clear the track! Soon she will be coming back!" She would sing this to herself after she was in bed, and before she had sung it through twice, she would be sound asleep.

In the morning there was packing to do. Eleanor had to be tidied up, so that the Westerners wouldn't make fun of her curly hair or say her frock was mussed. Honey

Bunch was so excited she could hardly eat her breakfast and she hardly heard the waiter when he said he hoped he should have the pleasure of serving her when she took the trip back.

They were due at Thompsontown at quarter to ten, and Honey Bunch was surprised that no one seemed to be bustling around or asking the conductor questions. On the train to Chicago, at every stop, a number of people had bumped down the aisles with their baggage and they had asked the porter and the conductor half a dozen questions apiece long before they came to the station where they got off.

"Everybody must know where Thompsontown is," said Honey Bunch to her daddy, as she sat quietly holding Eleanor.

They had left the door of the compartment open and Honey Bunch could see out into the car. No one seemed to be hurrying about.

"I think you'll find we are the only passengers whose tickets say Thompsontown," Mr. Morton replied. "This place is just a river landing and I doubt if any one else gets off. We take a boat next, Honey Bunch, and then an auto stage, and after that we finally come to the ranch."

Honey Bunch had not known they were to take a boat and now she gave a little bounce.

"Isn't it *fun?*" she cried.

The train was ten minutes late and it was almost ten o'clock when they felt the brakes slowing down the wheels. The porter had taken their bags and the conductor looked in to smile at Honey Bunch, who had come to know him very well during the last three days.

"The boat waits for the train—don't be uneasy, madam," said the conductor to Mrs. Morton. "Good-by, Honey Bunch."

"Good-by," Honey Bunch answered. "I've had a very nice time."

The conductor laughed, and then Honey Bunch and Daddy and Mother hurried out to the platform and down the steps, because you couldn't expect that long and important

train to make a very long stop at such a small
place. The porter took up his little step almost as soon as they were safely on the platform, but he stood out and waved to Honey
Bunch as the train began to move slowly
away.

"Doesn't look exactly like Chicago, does
it?" said Mr. Morton, as he saw Honey
Bunch staring at Thompsontown.

"Where are the *things?*" asked Honey
Bunch earnestly.

She meant the stores and the post-office and
the motion picture theaters and all the other
buildings that were built in Barham and in
greater numbers in the large cities.

"This is all the town there is," said her
daddy.

There was nothing but the station—and it
was like the water tank station, only there
wasn't even a water tank here—and a small
tin garage near it. The garage door was pad-
locked, but leaning against it was a little
brown-skinned man. He merely stared at
the strangers and said nothing.

"Where's the boat?" called Mr. Morton.

The man pointed. Honey Bunch looked where he pointed and saw a muddy, yellow stream that must be the river. There was a tiny steamer tied up at a narrow wharf and from the funnel the blackest smoke was coming in a great long cloud.

"Why doesn't he offer to carry the bags?" said Mrs. Morton in a low voice, as she and Honey Bunch followed Mr. Morton over to the wharf.

"I suppose he doesn't have to work and doesn't care to," Mr. Morton answered. "Don't let Honey Bunch stumble—my hands are full with this truck."

Honey Bunch had to be careful not to catch her foot in any of the loose boards, for the wharf, as soon as they stepped on it, seemed to shake and a loose board flopped up and rapped one of the leather bags smartly.

"Train's late—got to get under way," said a tall, thin man, reaching down from the deck of the steamer and lifting Honey Bunch up before she could say a word. "Dave, give the lady a hand, then cast off."

Mr. Morton threw both bags up on the deck and scrambled after them. The man called Dave had already helped Mrs. Morton up and had started to uncoil the heavy rope that fastened the steamer to one of the cross-pieces of the wharf. The black smoke came thicker and blacker, somewhere a shrill whistle sounded, and the boat began to move.

"Oh, Mother, look at the live chickens!" cried Honey Bunch, pointing to three crates on the forward deck.

CHAPTER XII

THE BOAT TRIP

THERE were white and black and brown chickens, sticking their heads out of the crates and apparently trying to see where they were going.

"Where's the egg crates, Dave?" bellowed the captain.

For a thin man he could make a great deal of noise, Honey Bunch decided. But she liked him. He had a little black and white dog that followed him everywhere and stopped and trudged on when he moved.

"Like my dog, Miss?" asked the captain, crossing the deck to speak to Honey Bunch, the little dog close at his heels.

"Oh, yes," Honey Bunch said eagerly. "What is his name?"

"High Tide," said the captain. "I got him last spring when the river ran pretty high

136

and some of the towns were flooded. He was nothing but a puppy then, but now he takes care of the boat for me when I'm away."

The captain seemed to like to talk and he said that his name was Binks—Captain Jonathan Binks.

"My daddy's name is David—like the other man's," Honey Bunch revealed.

"Is Dave's name David?" asked the captain, in great astonishment. "I never thought that, but likely enough it is. Where you folks landing?"

"We're to connect with the stage at Barton Landing, I believe," said Mr. Morton. "Our final destination is Three Rock Ranch."

"So?" Captain Binks ejaculated. "I heard the Tobins was looking for some people from the East. Those chickens are going to the ranch, and the empty egg crates. Tobin shipped in eggs last trip I took down river."

"What is the name of the river?" asked Honey Bunch.

"This is the Silver River," Captain Binks informed her. "Ought to have called it the Saffron River, to my way of thinking."

Honey Bunch didn't know what saffron was and her daddy explained that it is a yellow color.

"Where are all the other passengers?" she asked next.

Honey Bunch was having a very good time. Her daddy held her on the railing, for there was only one camp chair and of course her mother had that. The captain and Dave must have been used to standing up, Honey Bunch thought, or there might be a chair down in the engine room for them.

"You and your daddy and mother are all the passengers this trip," said Captain Binks. "There may be some folks waiting at Barton Landing. Not much travel this time of year —folks are pretty busy. High Tide and me like it first rate. In the spring the current is too strong and it keeps us poling, but when it's as it is now Dave and Custer can manage pretty well without me."

Honey Bunch wondered who Custer was and in a few minutes she found out. A colored man, dripping with perspiration, but wearing a bright red flannel shirt and a bow tie of green with white dots, came up on deck. He made a funny little bow when he saw the passengers and Mrs. Morton whispered that he must be Custer.

Captain Binks and his dog were standing near the cabin door, and the colored man stepped up to him and said something.

"Would you like to eat on deck?" bellowed the captain, turning to look at Mr. Morton. "Custer says it's pretty hot below."

"Oh, let's eat on deck," said Mrs. Morton.

So Mr. Morton said they would rather eat on deck than go below the deck, and Captain Binks shouted for Dave.

"You go down in the hold," he commanded, "and I'll take the wheel. Custer's got to cook."

It was very interesting, Honey Bunch thought, to see how the captain kept house on his boat. He took the wheel—which steered the steamboat, Daddy Morton explained—and Dave disappeared into the engine room. That was where the boiler was that made the steam which ran the boat, Daddy explained some more.

As for Custer, he must have had a kitchen somewhere, though neither Honey Bunch nor her mother could figure out where there was room for a kitchen on such a small boat. In less than twenty minutes, however, Custer bustled up on deck again with a crisp white coat over his very red shirt. He opened a small table and set it up and spread a clean white cloth over it.

"I didn't know we could get luncheon on the boat," said Mrs. Morton, smiling.

"Well, the captain doesn't do it every time, ma'am," Custer confided. "Some folks he lets take a chance. If the bus is late, there's a place in Barton landing where you can get coffee and sandwiches. But it's a messy place and when Captain likes his passengers he tells me to cook for 'em. The boat company want him to do it regular, but you can't make Captain do anything he don't want to do. No'm, Captain's right heady."

Custer was a good cook—Daddy Morton
said he hoped he was as good an engineer as
he was a cook—and he brought them up a
simple, but deliciously cooked hot luncheon.
There was a raspberry tart for Honey Bunch,
and High Tide came and sat by her while she
ate it, so she gave him a tiny piece and he was
most pleased with the attention.

Wherever Captain Binks and Dave ate, it
was not on deck, and as soon as the Mortons
had finished the table was cleared away.
Honey Bunch saw her daddy slip something
under his plate and when Custer cleared the
table he said "Thank you, sir—thank you
kindly, sir," a number of times. Honey
Bunch hoped he would buy himself a new
tie with the money, but she told her mother
that he might have thought a green and white
tie was pretty with a red shirt, and Mrs. Morton said she was afraid that was what Custer
did think.

There wasn't much to be seen from the
deck of the steamer—the land on both sides
of the river was "as flat as a pancake" Mrs.

Miller would have said. Even when they came in sight of Barton Landing, there wasn't much to be seen aside from a group of people on the wharf and a scattered cluster of buildings, apparently all facing on one street.

"The stage is over by the post-office," said Captain Binks. "Wait till I put down the gangplank, can't you?"

This last he said to a man who was so eager to come on board that he was trying to climb up the side of the boat.

Dave fastened the heavy rope around a post, put down the gangplank, and carried the two bags down for Mr. Morton. Then Honey Bunch's daddy took her in his arms, and Dave helped her mother and they marched safely ashore.

"Don't forget the chickens," said Honey Bunch, looking up at Captain Binks over her daddy's shoulder.

"I won't," he promised.

"You folks going on the stage?" said a friendly voice.

Honey Bunch stopped looking at the cap-

tain and Dave and Custer, who were lifting
the crates of chickens ashore, and turned to
stare at the owner of the voice.

My goodness, if Norman Clark could have
seen him!

"Are you a cowboy?" said Honey Bunch
in some awe.

The cowboy blushed. He had a very
brown skin, but you could see the red creeping under it. He was dressed exactly like
the pictures of cowboys Honey Bunch had
seen and he jingled when he walked.

"I'm a ranch hand," he said. "Tim Tobin
told me to keep an eye out for you. The
stage is over this way."

He picked up the two bags before Mr.
Morton could say a word and stalked across
the street.

"There's the stage!" said Honey Bunch
excitedly.

Mrs. Morton looked at it a little doubtfully. It was a rusty affair, and a man was
pouring water in the radiator. There seemed
to be a good many people inside and the top

was piled high with boxes and bags and fruit and vegetable and egg crates.

"Do you suppose there is room for us?" asked Mrs. Morton.

"Yes, ma'am, you go right ahead," Dave encouraged her. "They'll get you in."

Dave and Custer were struggling with the chickens in the crates, and when they reached the auto stage the driver stopped pouring in water and helped them hoist their freight to the top of the bus.

"Got a lady here," said Dave. "And a little girl and Mr. Morton. Some of you boys get up and let company have your seats."

Half a dozen cowboys scrambled out of the bus and stood grinning.

"We mustn't take your places," protested Mrs. Morton. "Isn't there another stage w could wait for?"

"Only one trip a day, ma'am," said the driver. "Here's a good place by the window. That lazy Bud Harris needn't think he can have all the fresh air. Tim Tobin said you

was coming to-day. Here's another seat—
move over, you Fred."

"I can take the little girl up front with
me," said the cowboy who had first spoken to
the Mortons. "Would you be afraid to ride
with me, Sis?"

"No-o, perhaps not," Honey Bunch said
shyly.

"He's a mighty nice fellow when you get to
know him, Sis," said the driver. "Well, all
aboard, everybody who's going with me. I
don't aim to waste any more of my time in
this me-tropolis."

Mrs. Morton said she would hold Honey
Bunch on her lap, but the stage was crowded
and stuffy and Honey Bunch knew her
mother was tired. She could tell when
Mother was tired, just by looking at her.

"I'll ride up front, Mother," decided
Honey Bunch.

"That Buck Dickson always has all the
luck," growled the cowboy the driver had
called Fred.

Buck Dickson took his seat next to the

driver, lifted Honey Bunch to his lap, and the stage started with such a roar and a spurt and a lurch that you would have thought all the inhabitants of Barton Landing would have rushed to the door to see what was the matter.

But Barton Landing was a very small town. Honey Bunch saw a post-office, a store, an auto repair shop, a blacksmith shop and four horses, and that was all. And as the stage made the same racket every day, no one was alarmed.

"Suppose we get acquainted," suggested Buck Dickson pleasantly. "I'm Buck—you heard my name. He's Wally James driving this cart. In back of us are Fred Epper and Bud Harris and the Dasher twins, old man Knipe and Sticky Needles and Granite Johnson."

"I'm Honey Bunch Morton," said Honey Bunch politely. "My daddy is Mr. Morton and my mother is Mrs. Morton. We're going to Three Rock Ranch."

"So am I," Buck assured her. "You going to take up ranching?"

"Am I, Daddy?" called Honey Bunch.

"Not permanently," Daddy Morton replied. "We're getting acquainted with the West. Ask Mr. Dickson if he has ever been East."

"No, I don't know anything about that part of the country," answered the cowboy. "Say, Wally, didn't you drop something?"

"Long as she goes, I know I didn't drop anything I have to have," the driver said cheerfully.

Honey Bunch put her head out and looked back.

"I think you dropped a chicken," she said anxiously.

And when she said that, she remembered something else.

"Oh, Mother, I've lost Eleanor!" cried Honey Bunch.

CHAPTER XIII

THREE ROCK RANCH

"ELEANOR!" exclaimed Mr. Morton.

"Why, we had her on the boat!" Mrs. Morton said.

Wally James had stopped the bus.

"Is Eleanor your sister?" he asked Honey Bunch.

She had to laugh at that. She was sure no little girl would ever be so careless as to leave her sister on the boat, even though she might leave a doll.

"Eleanor is a doll," explained Mrs. Morton. "I'm afraid we have left her on the boat. Is there any way we can send word to Captain Binks?"

"I'll see him to-morrow," Wally James said. "He'll take good care of Eleanor. Most likely he'll have her wrapped up for me and I'll bring her back to the ranch."

"Meanwhile, we'll have to rescue the chickens," suggested Buck. "Come on, Fred and Bud—a little exercise will do you good."

He lifted Honey Bunch gently into his seat and he and the other two men climbed down and ran back to where the crate of chickens lay in the road. Honey Bunch, to her own surprise as much as any one's, suddenly climbed over the back of the seat and into her mother's lap.

"I want to stay with you," she whispered.

When Buck came back and had helped hoist the crate to the roof of the car again— none of the chickens were hurt, he reported— he stared at the empty place beside the driver.

"Aren't you going to ride with me?" he asked Honey Bunch.

"I would rather not," she said, holding fast to her mother's hand.

Buck said nothing, but as Wally started the car, Bud Harris laughed.

"I always said your face would scare a kid into fits, Buck," he snickered.

The other men laughed loudly and Honey

Bunch saw the red creeping up into Buck's brown face.

She looked at Bud Harris. He wasn't trying to be mean, but he liked to tease people, Honey Bunch thought. She remembered that Albert Barnes was like that and sometimes Norman Clark. Perhaps Bud had been the kind of boy who liked to tease people and when he grew up to be a man he couldn't stop.

"I want to ride with Mr. Dickson, Mother," whispered Honey Bunch.

The cowboy heard her and turned around, his face positively beaming.

"You call me Buck, and you can have my best pony," he declared. "Up you go—there!"

He lifted her very gently over the back of the seat, and settled her comfortably on his lap.

"You and I," he told her, "are good friends. Any time you want some of these trifling ranch hands ducked in the horse trough, let me know and I'll oblige you."

"Oh, I wouldn't want them ducked in the

horse trough," said Honey Bunch hastily. "Have you a pony, Mr. Dick—Buck, I mean?"

"I've got the prettiest calico pony you ever saw in your life," said Buck proudly. "Wait till you see Star."

Honey Bunch thought that was a pretty name, and said so. She asked more questions about Star as the bus rattled along and presently the men inside began to drop off as they reached cross roads or came to the ranches where they lived.

Buck Dickson was the only one from Three Rock Ranch, and after half an hour's ride, he stood up and said he guessed they'd better be going.

"Some of you give me a hand with the chicken crates," he ordered.

Bud Harris helped him lift them down, while Honey Bunch and her mother and daddy waited. Bud lifted down their bags, too, and then the bus drove on.

"We'll leave the chickens till Jim drives down for them," said Buck. "Let me take

the bags. There's the house; you see you
haven't far to walk."

Honey Bunch looked ahead. She saw a
low, rambling house, set in a yard that had
a high fence all round it of chicken wire. A
porch seemed to be built on all sides of the
house and there was a porch swing and some
gay-colored rugs.

There was another house a little farther
away, and two or three men were sitting on
the steps. But there was no one to be seen
near the first house.

"Perhaps they're not at home," said Honey
Bunch, who really didn't know what she expected to see.

"Tobin's home, but he can't get around
very lively," Buck answered, setting the bags
down on the porch with a thump.

Instantly a girl about fourteen years old
came to the main door and she unhooked the
screen.

"Mother thought she heard the bus. Come
right in," she said cordially. "I'm Nettie
Wilcox."

Honey Bunch followed her mother and daddy into a large room which was hall and parlor and living room, library and workshop all in one, apparently, for the gray-haired, sunburned man who came limping forward to greet them. Buck had disappeared.

"Well, Morton, so you got here. I'm mighty glad to see you," sad the lame man. "We're in something of a mess, but now you've come things will straighten out."

Mr. Morton introduced the lame man to his wife as Mr. Tobin. Mr. Tobin told Honey Bunch he had a little niece who looked like her. Then Nettie Wilcox came back and took the travelers into a cool, clean bedroom, next to a comfortable bathroom, and told them that supper would be ready in half an hour.

"Isn't there any upstairs?" asked Honey Bunch as her mother brushed her hair for her.

Daddy Morton had gone to talk to Mr. Tobin—"about business"—Mrs. Morton said, and Honey Bunch had plenty of time to ask questions.

"I think the house has only one floor," replied Mrs. Morton. "See, Honey Bunch, there's Buck with a horse."

Honey Bunch ran to the window. There stood a horse with a saddle on him and Buck Dickson was holding the bridle.

"Is it his horse?" asked Honey Bunch.

"I rather think it is Mr. Tobin's horse," Mrs. Morton answered. "He has been trying to run this ranch for Daddy's friend, George Anchor, and I know from what Daddy told me he is most anxious to get back to his own place. Yes, he's going now."

They saw Mr. Tobin come limping out and Buck helped him mount the horse. Evidently his lameness did not interfere with his riding, for he urged the horse into a smart trot and a cloud of dust marked the road he followed.

"Supper!" called Nettie outside the bed-room door.

Honey Bunch was much surprised to find

that Nettie had a mother. Mrs. Wilcox was waiting in the dining room, and she apologized for not appearing before.

"I thought you'd be tired and I knew Tim Tobin would want to have a talk with Mr. Morton," she said; "so as long as I had a cake in the oven I thought you wouldn't care. Sit down while things are hot and Nettie will wait on you."

The dining room was furnished like the rest of the house—neatly and plainly. Nettie brought them in a well-cooked hot dinner, and, though she seemed a silent girl, she answered any question put to her readily enough. She told Honey Bunch's daddy that Mr. Tobin lived fifteen miles away and that he was lame as a result of having a horse fall on him when he was a young man.

"His own place is at sixes and sevens, while he's been here," said Nettie. "He certainly was glad when Mr. Anchor wrote you'd be out this summer."

Honey Bunch rather wanted to see Buck's pony that night, but by the time dinner was

over it was beginning to grow dark. Nettie
had told them that the ranch hands slept and
ate in the other house and they could hear
a guitar while they were still at the table.
When they went out on the porch, the men
were singing and Honey Bunch fell asleep
in her mother's lap, listening to a chorus
singing "Suwannee River."

The next day, bright and early, she began
to get acquainted with ranch life. Her daddy
was very busy and he and Buck rode for
miles, but Nettie was ready to take Honey
Bunch around. Honey Bunch decided to
ask her what she thought about a pistol for
Norman, as soon as she had a chance.

"Have you ever been on a ranch before?"
asked Nettie when, after dinner, she and
Honey Bunch set out together.

"No, but I've been on a farm," said Honey
Bunch. "My cousin, Stub, lives on a farm.
Isn't a ranch like a farm?"

"It's different," Nettie declared. "My
mother lived on a farm back East when she
was a girl. She always talks about the dairy

and her father was called a big farmer because he kept two men. Why, this ranch has
fifteen or twenty men when it's being run
right."

"Isn't it being run right now?" asked
Honey Bunch, for Nettie didn't sound al-
together pleased.

"It isn't being run at all," Nettie declared.
"The men are doing just as they please and
some of them have left. But come on and see
the horses. We may not have as many cows
as Eastern farms do, but I'll bet we have three
times as many horses."

Honey Bunch thought so, too. There were
all kinds of horses, it seemed to her, in the
enclosure which Nettie told her was a cor-
ral. Honey Bunch had to practice pronounc-
ing the word and when she finally could say
it she knew she had something to tell Norman
Clark.

"We've got more horses out on the range,"
explained Nettie, climbing up on a great
barred gate to pat the rough neck of a shaggy
little pony. "The cattle are grazing, too.

That's where Buck is taking your father. I'll bet you've eaten beefsteak back East that came from some of our steers."

There wasn't anything about the ranch or on it that Nettie didn't know. She said she had lived there since she was two years old and that her mother had been the housekeeper for Mr. Anchor before he had gone to Africa.

"He owns this ranch, you know," said Nettie. "He thought Red Pooly would stay till he came back from his trip, but he was the worst foreman we ever had. Finally he just left without a word to any one."

Nettie talked all the time now that she was alone with Honey Bunch. She told the little girl that when there was school, she rode the three miles on her own horse and she showed him to Honey Bunch and offered to let her have a ride.

"He's too high," objected Honey Bunch.

"Here comes Buck on Star!" Nettie exclaimed. "Star is gentle. You try her and you'll be crazy about riding."

Buck's pony was a beautiful little creature, with great soft eyes, a white nose and a brown and white skin, "put on in patches," Honey Bunch told her mother. There was a queer mark on her hip, and Buck said that all the horses and cattle were marked like that.

"Then we know they belong to Three Rock Ranch," he explained. "We can't keep our stock in fenced fields out here and we have to mark them to keep them from getting mixed up with other ranch stock."

"The stage is coming," said Nettie quickly.

"Let's you and me ride down and meet the bus, Honey Bunch," Buck suggested. "Up you go! There now, you can tell your friends back home that you're a real Western girl."

"Don't—let—Star rock!" begged Honey Bunch.

CHAPTER XIV

BUYING PRESENTS

BUCK laughed when Honey Bunch said that.

"Star can't rock," he said. "She's the best-gaited piece of horseflesh in this county. Wait till you see her canter."

He gave a queer little chirping noise, and Star pricked up her pretty ears. Then she broke into a gentle loping run that hardly jounced Honey Bunch at all.

"Nothing jerky about that, is there?" asked Buck proudly. "I told you Star is a wonder. And gentle! Say, that horse wouldn't step on a sand flea, if she saw it in time."

Honey Bunch's cheeks grew pink and her yellow hair stood out in the breeze. Already she liked Three Rock Ranch and was glad she had come.

160

The bus was waiting for them, and the driver, Wally James, had brought the lost Eleanor to her little mother.

"Captain Binks said to tell you that he had a scare when he saw the doll on the deck," said Wally. "He thought some mother had gone off and forgotten her baby."

Honey Bunch and Buck and Eleanor rode up to the house in state and Mrs. Morton and Mrs. Wilcox came out to see how well Honey Bunch could ride.

"Give me a week, and I'll have her as good a rider as Nettie," said Buck. "Star likes children and Honey Bunch can ride her anywhere and never be afraid of falling off."

Mr. Morton was working at the desk in the living room, going over papers Mr. Tobin had left for him, but he called that he was going to get the camera and take a picture of Honey Bunch on Star.

"I could send it to Ida Camp—or to Norman Clark, couldn't I?" said Honey Bunch. "I think it would look better if I had a pistol, though."

Nettie stared at her.

"A pistol?" said Buck.

"The boys in Barham want pistols," Honey Bunch explained. "They asked me to bring them some from the West."

"Oh, for souvenirs?" asked Nettie.

"Yes—for to-keep-souvenirs," and Honey Bunch nodded.

"You can get nicer things from the Indians. I'll take you over Saturday and let you see," promised Buck. "Pistols are pretty heavy, and I think a string of wampum would be better, myself."

Honey Bunch didn't know what wampum was, but before Buck could describe it, Mr. Morton came out with the camera and Honey Bunch and Star had their pictures taken. Star behaved beautifully and stood as still as a marble horse. Honey Bunch's daddy snapped her sitting in the saddle and standing on the ground beside Star and then he took Buck's picture, too, because Honey Bunch was sure Norman Clark would like to see a real cowboy.

"Take Nettie's picture, please, Daddy,"
begged Honey Bunch. "I want Ida Camp
to see Nettie." So Nettie had her picture
taken.

Later in the week Honey Bunch and
Nettie and Buck went over in the stage and
left the pictures to be developed at the drug
store. Every single one of them came out
well and Honey Bunch sent a set to Ida and
another to Norman, because she didn't want
them to have to wait until she came home
to know that she was having a good time at
Three Rock Ranch.

But before they went to town to take the
pictures and see the Indians there was a dust
storm that surprised Honey Bunch, who had
never seen one. It happened when Nettie
was sewing on the porch one morning.
Nettie had taken a great fancy to Eleanor
and had planned to make the doll a dress.
She was sewing, and Honey Bunch was
helping her by threading the needles and
finding the scissors when they would get
lost.

Suddenly a great gust of wind seemed to blow through the front yard.

"I have to shut the windows!" exclaimed Nettie, jumping up and running into the house.

She and her mother flew around, closing every window. Honey Bunch and her mother did not know what was coming, but Nettie did. She closed all the doors and banked sofa pillows across the front windows. Mr. Morton and Buck were out riding somewhere on the ranch, and Nettie said they would probably make for the nearest barn.

The wind continued to blow, but not a drop of rain fell. Instead, while Honey Bunch watched, great clouds of dirt and dust swept toward the house. In spite of the sofa cushions, the dust sifted in around the windows and under the doors. Some even got into Honey Bunch's blue eyes.

"I'm thankful we are not out in it," said Mrs. Morton. "I should think the grit would cut a man's face if he rode through a storm like this."

"Folks stop," Nettie explained. "The horses brace themselves and close their eyes and the men try to shelter themselves under their blankets. I don't mind a dust storm much, except you have to clean the whole house afterward."

And when this storm was over that was just what Nettie and her mother had to do. There was dust on all the furniture and dirt on all the floors. They had to dust and mop and shake the window curtains and Mrs. Wilcox said that when she lived on a farm in the East they never had dust storms.

When Honey Bunch's daddy came in to dinner—which was served at noon—he said that he and Buck had been near one of the cattle shelters, built to protect the steers in the winter time, and they had stayed there till the storm passed. Honey Bunch by this time knew what a steer looked like. They had short horns and they always kept moving, she told her mother to write Mrs. Miller.

Saturday afternoon Buck took Honey Bunch to town as he had promised. Nettie

went with them and they took the bus. Barton Landing was a little livelier on Saturday
than it was during the week, but you could
not call it a large town, no matter what day
you visited it.

"There are the Indians," said Nettie, as
they came out of the drug store, after leaving
the roll of film to be developed and printed.

Honey Bunch was disappointed. She had
thought Indians wore bright-colored blankets and plenty of strings of beads and, above
all, feathers in their hair. These Indians,
that is the men, wore clothes like Buck's, only
much dirtier. There were two women and
they had on calico wrappers, tied about the
waist with old knitted mufflers. If they had
any beads on, they did not show.

Buck had explained to Honey Bunch that
wampum was the money the Indians used to
use and that long ago these strings of shells
had been the only kind of dollar bills and
nickels and pennies and dimes the Indians
had known.

"Have they wampum now?" asked Honey

Bunch, looking at the Indians who were, sad
to relate, sitting on the curbstone before the
post-office, with their feet in the gutter, eating bananas.

"They don't use it now. They want good
American money, of course," said Buck.
"But they have all that kind of truck for sale.
I'll tell old Eagle Peak here to bring some
stuff out to the ranch next week. Your
mother might like to see their rugs and blankets."

"They won't come," Nettie declared.
"They're still afraid of Red Pooly."

But Buck went over to the Indians and
began to talk to them, waving his arms and
pointing his fingers, as though he thought
gestures might help them to understand
English.

"Didn't Red Pooly like Indians?" asked
Honey Bunch, watching Buck intently.

"Red didn't like anything," Nettie told
her. "He was the crossest man I ever saw.
The Indians used to come out to the ranch
the days when the men were paid off and try

to sell them trinkets. They never did any harm that I could see, but Red used to chase them off the place. Here comes Buck. I wonder what he told them?"

"They'll come out next Tuesday," reported the smiling Buck. "Eagle Peak is going to see to it that the squaws bring blankets, beads, moccasins and some rugs. He doesn't go around selling, but I'll bet he takes the money."

"Buck doesn't chase Indians, does he?" said Honey Bunch, when they were back on ranch.

"Buck doesn't chase anything," Nettie answered. "He's too easy-going for his own good. The men walk all over him."

The next morning Honey Bunch watched carefully, but she saw no one walking on any one else. When she mentioned this to her daddy he laughed and said that Nettie must have meant that Buck didn't make the men work as hard as they should.

"I like him," said Honey Bunch. "He laughs all the time. And he can sing, too."

Buck was usually laughing or singing or whistling, Honey Bunch had noticed. When the Indians came out to the ranch Tuesday, Buck helped to interpret and he was as interested in the things Honey Bunch's mother and daddy said she might buy for the children Honey Bunch knew, as though he were Norman Clark.

Honey Bunch selected different colored beads for the girls. Mrs. Morton said she though it was a good idea to get the same kind of gift for each girl. For the boys there were, as Buck had suggested, strings of wampum.

"The kids out here have great fun, using the wampum to trade with," said Buck, who seemed greatly pleased that Honey Bunch liked his choice of a present. "This Norman Clark you talk about can trade wampum for stamps or butterflies, or anything else he may be collecting."

For Mrs. Miller, Honey Bunch bought a little beaded purse. She selected a book of pressed wild flowers for Stub who, in spite of her careless ways, was a great outdoor girl and had a fair-sized flower collection that she had made all herself.

These presents were put away, together with a blanket and two small rugs Mrs. Morton had bought for her friends, and Honey Bunch agreed that they were very nice gifts indeed.

There was so much to do that the days seemed to fly by and two weeks had gone before Honey Bunch found time to go with Nettie to see her schoolhouse. It was a pretty long walk, but Nettie said they would walk slowly and rest before they came back, and she was sure Honey Bunch would like to see where she went to school.

Honey Bunch had some freckles on her nose now, from being out so much in the sun, and her hands were as brown as Nettie's. Her daddy told her she was getting fat, too, and Buck weighed her on the big scales and it was discovered that she had gained two pounds.

"If you gain a pound a week, perhaps

you'll outgrow your dresses before we go home," said her daddy.

But Mrs. Morton said she didn't think Honey Bunch would get as fat as that.

The road that led to the schoolhouse was not the main road, but a narrow, weedy trail about as wide as one automobile or wagon would need. Nettie usually rode to school in the winter, but though Mr. Morton was sure she could ride well, he said he would rather she didn't take Honey Bunch on a horse with her unless some one older could go with them. As every one was busy this morning, Nettie and Honey Bunch had to walk.

"Here comes some one," said Nettie suddenly, shading her eyes with her hand. "His horse isn't much. I never saw that outfit before."

Nettie sometimes talked just as Buck did, and Honey Bunch couldn't always understand what she meant. She knew, however, that this time Nettie was saying that the horse and rider who were coming toward them did not belong on any of the near-by ranches.

"Why—" said Honey Bunch, staring in astonishment. "Why, Nettie, *I* know that outfit!" and to Nettie's surprise, Honey Bunch began to run toward the solitary rider.

"It's Mr. Billy Slade!" she called as she ran.

CHAPTER XV

AN OLD FRIEND AGAIN

NETTIE had heard of Mr. Billy Slade. Indeed, Honey Bunch had told her everything that had happened on the journey from Barham to Chicago and from Chicago to the ranch. But she certainly had never expected to see Mr. Billy Slade riding a dejected-looking horse on this trail.

"I thought you said he went to some other place!" called Nettie, as Honey Bunch continued to run.

Their voices had reached the rider, who looked as dejected as his horse. He was slumped in the saddle, his chin sunk on his chest. Honey Bunch thought it was lucky there was no traffic on the road, because he didn't seem to be guiding the horse at all.

"Why, if it isn't my little lost girl!" cried Mr. Billy Slade, looking up when he saw the small figure running toward him. "You're not lost again, are you, Honey Bunch?"

"My, no!" Honey Bunch exclaimed cheerfully. "I'm not lost at all. This is Nettie Wilcox and she lives on Three Rock Ranch and we are going to see the schoolhouse where she goes to school."

Mr. Billy Slade took off his soft hat and made a bow to Nettie, who nodded rather awkwardly. She was shy with strangers.

"I'm glad to hear you're not lost," said Mr. Billy Slade. "But I might as well tell you that I am. That is, I started for Natalie and I've lost all sense of direction."

"Huh, Natalie's a little town over there," Nettie informed him, forgetting to be shy. "You took the wrong cross road. I guess the signs are down again. This road brings you out by our ranch and then you hit the main road that takes you to Barton Landing. You can get a boat there."

"He doesn't want a boat!" broke in Honey Bunch. "He's coming to see us! Daddy and Mother will be ever so glad to see you," she added sedately, turning to Mr. Billy Slade.

That young man looked undecided.

"I suppose I might stop for a few minutes," he said. "But look here, aren't you going to see some schoolhouse?"

"We don't have to go—Honey Bunch never walked that far, anyway, and I'm afraid she *would* be tired coming back," answered Nettie. "Is that your horse?"

"My best and only horse," Mr. Billy Slade assured her. "Not handsome, Miss Nettie, but dependable. Do you ride?"

"Some," said Nettie briefly.

Mr. Billy Slade swung out of the saddle.

"I wouldn't mind trying him," said Nettie. "I certainly like to ride a strange horse. What's his name?"

She scrambled into the saddle and the horse pricked up his ears. Perhaps he felt that here was a livelier rider than his first one—horses, you know, can feel the moods of their riders and many people believe they know when the people who ride them are grave or gay or afraid or happy.

At any rate the horse—"His name is Putter," Mr. Billy Slade called to Nettie—started off at a gentle gallop. Nettie was used to riding, and Honey Bunch knew she would not fall off.

"Where is your suitcase?" said Honey Bunch, slipping her hand into Mr. Billy Slade's and walking beside him just as they had walked together through the big railroad station in Chicago.

"My suitcase? Oh, I left that at the ranch till I can send for it," Mr. Billy Slade replied. "You see, I rode, and you can't pack a suitcase on Putter because he insists he wasn't meant for a baggage car."

"You mean you left your suitcase at the ranch where you went to work—the one you told Daddy about?" asked Honey Bunch. "Didn't you like it there?"

Though she was such a little girl, she was so interested in what her friends, little and big, did and thought and planned, that grown-up folk often talked to her as though she were older.

That was the reason Mr. Billy Slade, looking down into her blue eyes, said as simply as he would have told her daddy:

"Honey Bunch, that job was no earthly good."

Honey Bunch said "Oh!" and listened intently.

"I stayed long enough to work out my fare money and make a payment on this horse," went on Mr. Billy Slade. "Then I told them I was leaving. The owner of the ranch didn't have any cash—not enough to pay his hands or meet his debts from week to week. I would have felt sorrier for him if he hadn't been dashing around in two high-priced cars. His wife insisted on living in town and it took all the money he could scrape together to pay for those living expenses. The men took their pay in stock, some of them, and some, like me, bought a horse. But I yearned to have regular wages paid on regular time, so I had to leave."

Honey Bunch thought this over a minute.

"How could he dash around in two cars?" she wanted to know.

"Well, he dashed in one and his wife dashed in the other," explained Mr. Billy Slade, laughing.

Nettie had turned and now came back to them, her face flushed from exercise and excitement.

"Say, this Putter would be all right if he had a little more to eat," she told Mr. Billy Slade frankly. "I could fatten him up for you—or Buck Dickson could. Buck knows how to take care of a horse."

"Who is Buck Dickson?" asked Mr. Billy Slade.

"He's the foreman," said Nettie carelessly.

Nettie made Putter walk the rest of the way, and when they reached the ranch she rode him straight off to the barn. But Honey Bunch and Mr. Billy Slade went on to the house.

Honey Bunch knew where to find her daddy—if he was in the house. She made straight for the long living room, taking Mr.

Billy Slade with her. He suggested that perhaps he'd better wait on the porch, but Honey Bunch was determined not to let go his hand.

"Daddy!" she cried, as soon as she saw her daddy seated at the desk. "Daddy, look! Here's Mr. Billy Slade!"

Mr. Morton glanced up from his papers and then jumped to his feet.

"Well, well!" he said. "I am certainly glad to see you, Slade!"

The two men shook hands and Mr. Billy Slade explained that Honey Bunch had found him this time.

"I had no idea I was in the section where you were," he told Mr. Morton. "I never had a bigger surprise in my life than when I saw Honey Bunch running toward me. By the way, how is Eleanor?"

So he had remembered the name of Honey Bunch's doll! Eleanor's little mother beamed upon him and told him that Eleanor was very well indeed and was sitting in the porch swing at that moment.

"Sit down and let's bring things up to date, Slade," said Honey Bunch's daddy. "Seems to me you look a little thinner than you did."

Honey Bunch curled up in one of the big chairs. She could be as quiet as a little mouse and she never interrupted to ask questions, even when her daddy talked about things that she did not understand. That was the reason no one said "run away and play," to Honey Bunch; she could listen without bothering grown-up folk.

Mr. Morton talked to Mr. Billy Slade for half an hour and for half an hour Honey Bunch listened silently. It seemed that the ranch where the young man had worked owed a great deal of money, not only to its employees but to storekeepers and other ranchmen.

"In a way, I suppose I was a fool to leave," said Mr. Billy Slade, "because I had a place to sleep and three meals a day as long as I stayed there. But there was no prospect that things would ever be straightened out and if it came to a sheriff's sale I didn't see much prospect of the help being paid off while there was a pile of other debts to be presented."

"Then you're out of a job and with no money saved?" Mr. Morton suggested.

Honey Bunch sat up a little straighter.

"Daddy," she said, speaking very rapidly, "he used to be a foreman, why couldn't he be a foreman here?"

"But there is a foreman here," Mr. Billy Slade said, smiling. "Buck somebody or other—Nettie mentioned him."

Honey Bunch looked anxiously at her daddy. Was Buck the foreman, really?

"I'm trying to get things into shape for my friend who owns this ranch, Slade," said Mr. Morton slowly. "He's in Africa and won't be back for at least another year. The place does need a foreman. Buck Dickson holds the job nominally since the man Anchor hired left. But Buck is too good-natured and easy-going. He can't control the men, and though they like him they override his orders frequently. I'm wondering whether you wouldn't be a good man to put in. What about references?"

Mr. Billy Slade reached into his coat pocket and brought out several papers.

"You could investigate these," he said. "They're from ranches where I have worked. Of course I wasn't foreman except at this last place, but I handled as many men and did practically the work of the foreman in several jobs. I'd be glad to have you write to these men."

"I will—right away, too," promised Mr. Morton. "Meanwhile, I see no reason why you shouldn't hold the place temporarily. We'll go out and interview Buck."

Honey Bunch went, too. Buck Dickson was glad to see Mr. Billy Slade and said so. Buck confided that he hated responsibility and that he knew the men took advantage of him.

"They're a good crowd, but they don't pay any attention to me," was the way he put it.

Though Honey Bunch didn't know exactly

when it all happened, in the next two weeks
her daddy had written to the names and ad-
dresses Mr. Billy Slade had furnished him
and had heard from the ranch owners for
whom he had worked. They approved of
him and gave him a high rating, one or two
saying that if they had not already had fore-
men who had worked years to get the position, they would have liked to employ Mr.
Billy Slade in that capacity.

"Will he be foreman, Daddy?" asked
Honey Bunch, a few days before the Mortons were to start on their trip East.

"Here's the letter to George Anchor," her
daddy answered, holding up a letter he had
just stamped and sealed. "In it I'm telling
him that I am going back home, leaving
Three Rock Ranch in full and complete
charge of Billy Slade. In these last two
weeks he has taken hold of both the business
end and the outdoor work so intelligently
that I feel the ranch is in better shape than
it has been for years. It was lucky for us
and for Mr. Anchor that you fell over Billy

Slade's suitcase that day, Honey Bunch."

Of course this made Honey Bunch perfectly happy. She told Mr. Billy Slade so. And he said he was perfectly happy, too.

He came to the boat landing to see them off and so did Buck Dickson and Nettie Wilcox and her mother. Every one of them begged Honey Bunch to come back to the ranch and see them again soon. But before that could happen, the little girl was to have another interesting vacation. It is called, "Honey Bunch: Her First Summer on an Island."

"I have to see Mrs. Miller and Lady Clare and Ida and Norman," said Honey Bunch earnestly, "and tell them about the West. But after that perhaps I can come and see you some more—unless you all come and see me."

So it was left that way and the boat started upstream, taking Honey Bunch and her daddy and mother toward home.

THE END